Granny Forks a Fugitive

(A Fuchsia, Minnesota Mystery)

by

Julie Seedorf

This book is fiction. All characters, events, and organizations portrayed in this novel are the product of the author's imagination or are used fictitiously. Any resemblance to actual persons—living or dead—is entirely coincidental.

Copyright 2015 by Julie Seedorf

All rights reserved. No parts of this book may be reproduced or transmitted in any form or by any means, electronic or mechanical, including photocopying, recording or by any information storage and retrieval system, without written permission from the author, except for the inclusion of brief quotations in a review.

For information, email **Cozy Cat Press**, cozycatpress@aol.com or visit our website at: www.cozycatpress.com

ISBN: 978-1-939816-69-6

Printed in the United States of America

Cover design by Paula Ellenberger
http://www.paulaellenberger.com/

1 2 3 4 5 6 7 8 9 10

Acknowledgements

Thank you to Boneyard Coffee and Tea in Champagne, Illinois, for allowing Granny to drink their specialty coffee at the Pink Percolator.

Also thanks to author Barbara Jean Coast allowing me to mention her book, *A Nate To Remember* as one of Granny's reading pleasures.

Memories are always front and center when I write, and this book was not any different. I had to include Hanson Drugstore and their soda fountain and Whirlawhip machine that was so much a part of my life growing up and also in my early adult years when I actually got to operate the machine—sometimes with a little complaining. It was complicated and messy to clean, but those Whirlawhips were yummy to eat.

I also would like to thank my publishing company, Cozy Cat Press, and editor Patricia Rockwell for believing in me.

I dedicate this book to my family. Families are occasionally complicated and messy, but the love we feel for one another, never leaves us. I love you with all my heart.

CHAPTER ONE

The burlap bag, tied to a branch on the oak tree, bulky in size and swaying in the wind, was begging to be hit or punctured, so its contents would spill to the ground like confetti showering a celebration on those who stood below.

Hermiony raised the bat high over her head and took a swing, connecting with the unsightly, uneven bag. The bag moved but didn't break. She hit it again, harder. Still the bag refused to give up its contents.

Dropping the bat and picking up a stick that had fallen to the ground in the wind, Hermiony took a poke at the bag, tearing a small hole in its side. Still the contents stayed comfortably wrapped in the depths of the bag.

Putting the stick down, Hermiony backed up at an angle from the tree, and took a running leap. Her feet lifted her high enough off the ground so she was able to grab the bag where it had ripped from being poked with the twig. Her body hanging from the bag, she pulled hard, but the tree would not let go of the bag. It was a tug of war between Hermiony and the tree. Hermiony tugged and the tree tugged back. All the while, Hermiony's legs dangled in the wind as she tried to hold on and rip open the treasure inside of the bag.

Wisps as soft as feathers landed on Granny's face, whispering to her through her dream. She opened one eye and felt her arm above her head being pulled in the direction of the side of the room. Quickly opening the other eye, she noticed feathers dancing over her face, body, and bed. All of a sudden, her arm let go from whatever she'd been holding on to, and more feathers drifted down, creating a feather snowstorm in her bedroom.

Bleat! Bleat!

"Mrs. Bleaty!" Granny yelped as she sat up, realizing that she and Mrs. Bleaty, her goat, had been having a pillow fight while she'd slept, and that the pillow had won. Sitting up in bed, Granny grabbed the empty pillow casing away from Mrs. Bleaty.

"Why aren't you over at Silas Crickett's this morning badgering Radish?" Granny asked the goat. Usually, Mrs. Bleaty, Baskerville, and the shysters visited Franklin, Granny's fiancé, or Silas Crickett, Granny's neighbor, at this time of the morning.

Granny grabbed her cell phone and checked the time. She'd overslept. It was almost nine o'clock. *Must have been the wine and chocolates,* thought Granny. Grabbing the bedpost, she steadied her body before her feet hit the floor. Granny knew her single days were numbered and she cherished her evenings, relaxing in bed with her wine and chocolates, reading a good book, and wearing her risqué hot pink night clothes. Although she supposed when she got married, she might surprise Franklin once in a while with the nighttime attire she always purchased from *Red Hot Momma's Boutique*. However, it wouldn't do for it to be an *every night* kind of thing. She would save her nightwear for special occasions—such as when she did something Franklin might not approve of. Red Hot Momma's nighttime attire had a way of getting her her own way.

The cell phone that Granny held in her hand chimed *Lullaby, Goodnight, My Angel,* signifying that Angel was calling. Granny chuckled as she answered the phone. She and her new granddaughter had bonded from the moment they'd met.

"Morning, Angel; it's a little early for you, isn't it?"

"Granny, its 9:00 a.m., you have to come and help me! I'm in trouble! I can't find Thor and Mom. Hurry, Granny, hurry!" Granny heard the tears through the phone connection.

"I'll be right there as quick as a pig can jig."

Granny threw her phone down on the bed, looked at Mrs. Bleaty who'd climbed into the bed and was already snoozing, grabbed her robe to cover her Hot Momma pj's, and took off down the hall to get to the door.

Granny's feet came to a screeching halt when she encountered Angel in her living room.

"Angel, what are you doing here? Didn't you just call me and tell me you were in trouble? Didn't you just tell me that you couldn't find your mom and Thor?" Granny questioned. Maybe she'd imagined the phone call amidst all the feathers and the dreams.

"I did, Granny, I did." Angel gave a loud sniff.

Granny peered closely at Angel.

"Are you sure you're crying?"

"Oh, Granny, I looked and looked and Thor and Mom aren't here!"

"Why would you look here? Why would they be here?" Granny asked the almost-five-year-old little Angel, standing in the middle of her living room.

"I can't find them here because," Angel answered Granny innocently before calmly walking to the front door. "They're there!" Angel opened the door and held it wide open.

"Surprise! Surprise! Surprise!"

Granny jumped back and scowled at the intruders.

"Hi, mom! Happy Birthday!" Thor kissed his mother on the cheek while helping Heather, his pregnant wife and Angel's mother, into the house.

"You look great for your age," Granny's daughter Penelope stated from behind Thor as she and husband Butch hauled a big package through the doorway.

"Mom, may the stars align with your day." Granny's other daughter Starshine hugged her mother, at the same time motioning her fiancé, Lars, into the house.

Granny felt something alive and squirming put into her arms as she looked into her neighbor Silas Crickett's eyes. "Something lively to spice up an old, old, old woman's life!" said Silas, as he raised his eyebrows and kept on going further into the house. Granny looked down to see what he'd put in her arms. Before Granny could see what it was, the live, wiggling creature was taken out of Granny's arms and a pair of dangling red earrings made out of letters was placed in her hands. The words read, "You're mine!"

Granny looked up into Franklin Jester Gatsby's eyes just in time to see him wink as he grabbed her for a smacking good kiss. Granny tried to extricate herself from her fiancé's arms before anyone saw her blushing. Glancing behind Franklin and seeing the next reveler walk through her door, she wiggled out of his grasp. Handing the earrings to Starshine, she quickly pushed past Franklin to confront the new party goer.

"What's she doing here?" Granny asked, glaring at the newcomer.

Thor moved to his mother's side, not sure if he should grab hold of her arms in case she came out swinging. "It's her birthday too," he said.

Starshine moved close to the woman who was almost a clone of her mother. "We didn't want her to be alone on her birthday."

"She's your twin sister, Mom. It's been a lot of years since you both celebrated your birthdays together," Penelope reminded her mother with an apologetic look.

"Oh, for goodness sakes!" Silas Crickett piped in, "let the woman sit down; she's a lot frailer than you, Granny, and she might faint at your attitude."

Granny gave an appraising look at her twin sister Amelia before turning to Angel with a gleam in her eye. "Angel, you tricked me."

Angel jumped up and down in glee. "I did! I did! See, I can be tricky too. Just like you, Granny."

Before Granny had a chance to reply, the door opened again, and Mavis and George, her neighbors from across the street, along with her friend Delight, owner of the Pink Percolator, pushed a movable tray with a large cake on top of it into the house.

"It's June and we're going to croon; we'll make you swoon and none too soon; on this day that's not May; we'll shout hooray, because it's your birthday. June two is right for you. So don't be blue 'cause we've got a brew. Happy Birthday to you!" Delight and Mavis sang off-key as Granny's menagerie of animals—Fish, Little White Poodle, Tank, Furball, and Baskerville—chimed in, barking and meowing. Mrs. Bleaty, coming out of the bedroom to see what the commotion was, provided the bleats. The animal noises completed the song with the perfect background chorus.

"Don't you know it's not nice to surprise an old woman so early in the morning," Granny complained. "Might have given me a heart attack, especially with that terrible rhyme."

"Hermiony," Franklin said, taking her hand and leading her over to the couch where he sat her down. He then moved to Amelia who was standing silently in the corner of the room. "Amelia." Taking her hand, he led her over and indicated she should sit next to her twin sister.

Granny quickly scooted into the corner of the couch, eyeing Amelia warily.

Angel sidled up next to Granny and stared at the two sisters. "Don't you like each other, Granny? You told me I should be nice to everyone."

Granny cleared her throat, "Um, Um. Well, so I did."

"Are you scared of your sister, Granny? Is that why you don't want to sit next to her?" Angel asked in a puzzled tone.

The rest of the people in the room gave Granny knowing grins, and Thor raised his eyebrows, indicating with a nod of his head that he wasn't helping his mother get out of explaining this to Angel.

Granny turned to look at her twin sister, Amelia, who was silently listening to the conversation. In a soft voice, Granny acknowledged her sister's presence, "Happy Birthday, Amelia. It's been a long time."

"Too long, Hermiony, too long. Happy Birthday to you too," said Amelia. "I'm so happy to be sharing this time with you and your children. They're my family too, you know."

Granny turned away, a hurt look in her eyes but, noticing the questioning faces of the other people in the room, she quickly stood up. "Did ya think about coffee with that cake?"

Silas, seeing the hurt in Granny's eyes, moved forward. "I don't think they put enough candles on that cake for someone as old as you."

Granny skewered him with a look. "You old cantankerous coot, why are you here? Counting the candles to see if you think I'm going to kick the bucket soon?"

Delight giggled at Amelia's shocked look. "Don't worry Amelia; those two are always going at it. He's the male version of her; they just don't see it yet."

"And what was that wiggly thing you put in my hands?" Granny inquired of Silas.

Laughing, Silas answered, "I let it loose, but I'll give you a clue. It's silent as a mouse."

Granny turned to Baskerville, "Baskerville, don't you want to eat a *Radish*?" referring to Silas's gray parrot.

Heather, Penelope, and Starshine handed out cake while Delight poured everyone, except Angel, a cup of freshly brewed coffee from the Pink Percolator. The shysters and Baskerville licked up the crumbs on the floor. Mrs. Bleaty busily tried to break into the presents that the visitors had brought and left by the front door for Granny.

"Amelia, how is the factory you're building coming along?" Butch raised a piece of the Chocolate Raspberry Lemon Fudge Cake to his lips.

"George and I can't wait to try your chocolate, Amelia. Imagine having a chocolate factory in town!" Mavis said, making a smacking sound with her lips.

Before Amelia could answer, Angel dropped a small box in Granny's lap. "It's a present from my Grandpa. You've got to open it first, Granny. Please! Please!"

"Angel, you interrupted a conversation. Aunt Amelia was about to answer a question about her factory," Heather reminded her daughter.

"That's quite alright." Amelia's soft voice could barely be heard. "There's plenty of time to answer questions. I'm not going anywhere."

"Unfortunately," Granny stated under her breath.

"Did you say something, Hermiony?" Amelia asked. "I didn't quite hear that."

Granny, ignoring Amelia's comment, continued to unwrap the small box. Lifting the lid, she saw the glint of something pink. Granny took the tiny object out of the box.

Franklin bent down in front of her on his knee. "Hermiony Vidalia Criony Fiddlestadt, will you consent to marry me again?" referring to the fact that the Christmas wedding they had planned had gotten interrupted and postponed. "With this ring, I commit to accepting your colorful personality, your willful ways, and your sparkling independence. Let's start anew and say *I do*."

"What? No car this time?" Granny teased with a twinkle in her eye. The last time Franklin had proposed, he'd given her a red '57 Chevy Corvette convertible.

A loud crash interrupted Franklin's answer with pieces of cake landing on top of his head. Frosting spattered all over Granny's hair, and Baskerville's loud howl filled the air.

"Food fight! Food fight!" Angel chanted.

"Stop everyone! Stand still so you don't get cake all over the house!" Penelope yelled.

Granny, wiping the frosting out of her hair, looked up to encounter Silas smile.

"Whoops, Baskerville must have accidently knocked into the table." Silas gave Granny a shrewd look and said, "Happy Birthday, Hermiony!" He waved while walking out the front door.

Granny grabbed Franklin's arm, putting a stop to his attempt to brush the chocolate cake off his clothes. "I have an announcement to make!" Granny shouted, stopping all the commotion in the room.

Everyone stopped cleaning up the mess to listen to Granny. "I, Hermiony Vidalia Criony Fiddlestadt, accept Franklin Jester Gatsby's latest proposal!"

CHAPTER TWO

Holding on to a cup of coffee with her right hand, Granny lifted her left hand so she could get a better look at the pink diamond adorning her finger.

The ring was a good complement to the first engagement ring Franklin had given her that she still wore on the same hand and the same finger as the new one. "Yup, he staked his claim!" Granny mused to the empty room.

The party was over and Granny had some time to herself before she had to meet Mavis and Delight in the underground streets by Graves Funeral Home, per their instructions. She didn't know what they'd planned, but she knew it would be good.

Something scurried past her feet, brushing up against her ankle as it passed, and skittered underneath the arm chair across the room. Granny sat up, peered at the fluttering blanket, covering her chair and gently draping to the floor. *That ornery coot Silas wouldn't have left a mouse in her house, would he?*

The one thing that no one knew about Granny was that she was scared of mice. Tucking her legs underneath her in her chair, she remained still as she watched to see what was hiding under the armchair. Of course, if anyone else had been around, she would have blustered through. It wouldn't do any good to her reputation to let her family and friends know that the aging amateur sleuth was scared of mice. Well, she figured she'd just rest in her chair for a little while. One of the shysters or Baskerville, or Mrs. Bleaty, was sure to come back soon. They'd take care of the little creature hiding under the draped blanket of the arm chair.

Keeping a close eye on the blanket, Granny sipped her coffee. It had been quite a year. Looking again at the two rings on her finger, she thought perhaps fate was telling her that the problems she and Franklin had getting hitched, should have warned her off of accepting another ring and scheduling another wedding.

First, she'd been kidnapped, and when they could have gotten the show on the road again, she looked up straight into the face of her twin sister, Amelia. It had been such a shock that Granny had fainted dead away, thinking she'd seen a ghost. In all the excitement of her family seeing someone who looked just like her that they hadn't known about, and getting Granny to the Emergency Room to see Dr. Dreamboat in the ER, the wedding got postponed.

Granny's musings were interrupted when the four shysters romped into the house through their pet door. Little White Poodle stopped on a dime and gave a sniff in the air. Tank growled and pawed the carpet while sniffing at the armchair that Granny had been keeping her eye on.

Granny tucked her feet a little tighter under her as Fish and Furball gave a loud yowl and bounded to the chair in question, batting at something underneath.

Granny grabbed her cell phone that was in her pocket and shouted into it, "Crabby old man!" The phone placed a call.

"Hermiony, my Hermiony, do you want me to come and party with you?" A chuckle followed the question.

"Silas Crickett, you get over here and get whatever smarmy live creature you left here out of my house!"

"Why, Granny, you'd do anything to get me over to your house, wouldn't you? Do I smell a rat?"

"A rat? You left a rat over here?" Granny screamed into the phone, while pulling her feet back further into the chair.

A click could be heard on the other end of the line. At the same time, Furball dove under the chair and came up with something in her mouth. Granny moved further back in her chair as Furball, with a large white, wiggling rat dangling from her mouth, joined Granny on her chair.

"I don't need a present Furball," Granny said, cringing in alarm as the cat seemed to want to present the rat to Granny. At that same moment, the door opened, and Silas walked into the room, taking the rat from Furball's mouth and holding it in his arms. He winked at Granny.

Seeing the creature safely in Silas's arms, Granny jumped up and advanced on Silas. "You gave me a rat for my birthday! You rat! You could have given me a heart attack. That's what you were trying to do, wasn't it? Give me a heart attack so you could have my animals and my house! You want to live on the side of the street with the underground streets."

Granny stomped to the door and grabbed her umbrella. I'm going for a ride to cool off and when I get back you'd better be gone with that creature, or I'll have your son arrest you for terrorizing an old lady on her birthday!" Granny was referring to the fact that Silas's son, Ephraim Cornelius Stricknine, nicknamed by Granny the Tall Guy, was co-chief of police for the town of Fuchsia, along with Granny's son, Thor, the other part of the "co" in the "chief."

Silas flashed a wicked grin at Granny, "If you change your mind and want to claim your gift, you can find little Squeaky at my house with Radish."

"Lock up when you leave," Granny advised, slamming the door on her way out.

CHAPTER THREE

Granny headed across the yard to her new garage. This garage replaced the old garage that had been totaled in an arson fire the previous fall. This new garage had more character then the old one. Granny had decided that if she was going to build a new garage, it was going to be unique. This garage had a turret at the top where she could gaze at the stars at night, or watch her neighbors when the fancy hit her. She thought of it more as a disguised guard tower for the neighborhood. Once in the turret, she could see across the Fuchsia Cemetery that bordered her back yard.

It gave Granny a thrill to view her red '57 Chevy convertible that was parked once again in her garage, instead of being stored at Franklin's house. The car was an engagement gift from Franklin their first time around, replacing the two red '57 Chevy convertibles that had perished in the fire.

Sliding into the driver's seat, Granny adjusted the mirrors, started the car, and turned on the radio. Pushing the opener on the garage door, she eased the car out onto the driveway. Checking to make sure no one was watching, she gently backed onto the street. She brought the car to a complete stop. Granny once again looked around. The neighborhood was deserted. It was time to celebrate her birthday her way. The top was down; it was an 80 degree June day. The sun glinted on her windshield, sending its rays to shine right in Granny's eyes. Granny cranked up the radio as loud as it would go, pulled her sunglasses down over her eyes, and with one stomp on the gas, peeled out of her neighborhood and headed for the open road.

For some reason, her mind was filled with thoughts of Amelia. Why couldn't she have stayed out of their lives? Granny hadn't seen her twin since they were 18 years old—out of sight, out of mind. They'd all been instructed to never speak her name in their household ever, by their parents. Granny and her brothers had erased the name *Amelia* from their lives.

Deep in thought about her past, Granny didn't notice that her red Corvette knew exactly where to take Hermiony Vidalia Criony Fiddlestadt on her birthday. Before she knew it, the car turned into an abandoned farmhouse. Granny supposed she must have unconsciously headed to this spot. She hadn't been out to the old farm since her husband, Ferdinand, had died. It was the old home place where she and her brothers, Briony and Abraham, had grown up—along with her twin sister Amelia. After her parents had died, she and Ferdinand had moved their family here.

Granny took one look at the dilapidated old house and said to the air, "Lots of rats in there, I bet."

Opening the car door, Granny put her feet on the ground and lifted herself out of the car. Yup, the old trees from the apple orchards were still there in the distance, abandoned. It looked as if some of them could still be fruitful. Herman Picnic—if he hadn't croaked—would have had a field day stealing those apples with no one around to protect them. Granny chuckled, remembering the day when she was a young girl and got the best of Herman Picnic. She bet Herman still had no idea when he died, how the wagon had sunk so fast so many years ago, leaving him on the ground with a broken leg.

Making her way to the steps of the old house, Granny looked up to the second-story window. She could almost see her brother, Briony, hanging by one hand out the window the night he'd tried to jump from the house to the tree to sneak out to meet his girlfriend. Granny had already made the jump to the tree, so she could sneak out to the barn to get her late night snack of chocolate and donuts that she'd hidden in the hay loft earlier in the week. Granny remembered offering Briony a branch to grab, but only if he brought her some more chocolates and donuts back from town. He wouldn't, but she offered him the branch anyway. Just as he grabbed for the branch, she pulled it away and he tumbled straight to the ground with such a thunk that it brought their dad running. Well, she hid in the tree and had her chocolate and donuts that night, but her brother spent many hours in the barn cleaning something that looked a lot like chocolate but had an aroma that only a mother pig could love.

Now as she stared at it, the house didn't look safe. Granny looked around and saw that the silo seemed to still be in good shape. Moving through the silo door into the empty silo, she could smell the aroma of hay. The people who rented the property must have stored hay in the silo in the not too distant past, because there was still a pile by the wall of the silo.

Closing her eyes and breathing in the scent of the farm, Granny sat down on a barrel in the middle of the silo. Thoughts of Amelia and her parents swirled in her head. She hadn't thought about this place and its memories in many years. She could see through the window in the silo that it was getting late. She'd better hurry if she was to meet Mavis and Delight for their surprise. As she stood up, she tripped over a pitchfork lying on the ground. Picking it up, she studied it. *Hmm,* she thought, *this might make a good weapon.*

From shaking the pitchfork, it seemed sturdy. She wondered if the tines were still strong, so she walked over to the mound of hay and plunged the tines of the pitchfork into the mound. They struck something very solid. Granny pulled the pitchfork out and saw that the tines were tinged in red. Shocked, she backed away from the hay mound just as a hand that had been pulled out by the tines peeked through the hay.

"Okay, who's there playing a joke on me?" asked Granny. "Silas, did you follow me here? Come out!"

Granny held the pitchfork in the air ready to pounce on whomever came out of the mound, but it was silent and the hand lay still.

Reaching down, Granny touched the wrist that was attached to the hand. There was no pulse.

"Great! I haven't been back to the farm since Ferdinand died and now the hand of fate just happens to pop up out of a hay mound."

Granny reached for her phone. "Thor!" she shouted into the phone, making it dial her son's number.

"Hi, mom!" he answered, "are you celebrating?"

"You might say that. I think it's time at my age to confess. There's something I haven't told you."

"You're getting old?" Thor joked.

"I still own the farm. And there's a......there's a.....could be a dead body here?"

CHAPTER FOUR

Pacing up and down the driveway of the old farm place, Granny's feet moved slowly while she waited for the authorities to arrive. At one point, her footsteps hesitated at the silo door as she contemplated moving the hay off the arm and body of the person whose pulse no longer was beating.

Fear had never stopped Granny before from being inquisitive when facing a dead body, but now something held her back. Maybe it was the fact this was her home, even if she had left it years ago and had never looked back.

Hearing the sound of sirens, Granny moved to meet the cars coming down the long driveway. Thor hopped out of the first of the two fuchsia-colored police cars and ran to meet Granny. The Tall Guy exited the second car, taking his time to give a sweeping glance over the property.

"What are you doing here?" Thor asked his mother in an exasperated tone.

"What does it look like I'm doing here?" Granny countered. "Finding a dead body; shouldn't that have been your job?"

"What did you mean? You still own this place? We thought you'd sold it when we were kids. And now you're out here and someone's dead?" Thor asked.

"I was just taking a little drive on my birthday," replied Granny, "doing a little travel down memory lane. Thought I'd visit the old place. How was I to know John Doe was going to be here too?"

The Tall Guy, hearing the conversation, quickly interrupted, "They'll be time for that later. Thor, maybe you shouldn't be here since your mom is again involved in a murder." the Tall Guy turned to go into the silo.

Granny, hearing the word *murder*, jumped straight in front of the Tall Guy before Thor could stop her, tapping the Tall Guy hard in the chest with her finger. "I'm not involved in a murder!" Granny shouted, upset at hearing the word *murder* and *involved* in the same sentence. "I'm involved with a dead person. There's a difference. You said the word *murder* without facts. It could just be a normal dead person."

Thor lifted Granny out of the way and followed the Tall Guy into the silo. At that moment, another car drove up, revealing Franklin Jester Gatsby. "What are you doing here?" Granny shouted to him as he exited his car. Not waiting for an answer, Granny disappeared through the silo door.

Inside, she saw that Thor was holding the pitchfork that Granny had dropped on the ground. "There's blood on this pitchfork," Thor noted while watching the Tall Guy gently move the hay off the body.

"Ah, um, I can explain that," Granny said in a hesitant voice, but her statement was lost to Thor who knelt down next to the body that the Tall Guy had uncovered.

"He's been stabbed in the arm by the pitchfork," Thor remarked. The Tall Guy joined Thor, getting down on both knees, to examine the body.

"He hasn't been here too long—maybe a few hours. Do you know him?" the Tall Guy questioned Thor as Franklin came in the door and moved next to Granny.

"Can't say that I do," said Thor. "Want to tell us what happened, Mom?" Hearing no answer, he turned to look at Granny. She seemed frozen to the spot with an incredulous look on her face.

"Hermiony," Franklin said, putting his arm around Granny and giving her a hug and a little shake at the same time. "Are you okay? Hermiony?"

All three men waited for an answer.

Granny still stood frozen to the spot. Thor stood up, facing his mother. "This has been too much of a shock; maybe we should take her to see Dr. Dreamboat in the ER."

Granny shook off Franklin's arm and moved past Thor, closer to the body. "I can hear you. Arrest me! I killed him! I forked him with the pitchfork, but I didn't know he was here! Really, I didn't! I'm ready for the orange jumpsuit."

As if mesmerized, Granny knelt down next to the body and stroked the unknown man's face.

Thor, the Tall Guy, and Franklin appeared to be intruders on a private moment, even though they had no idea what was so mesmerizing for Granny about the dead body.

Finally, Franklin gave a short cough to break the silence. "Hermiony, let's go down to the police station and you can tell us what happened. Do you know who this is?"

Granny took one last look at the face of the man lying dead in the hay before turning to answer. "He was the love of my life! I forked the love of my life!" She dropped her head, her eyes fixated on the floor.

Silas Crickett, hearing Granny's last words as he entered the silo, walked over and stared down at the dead man, making a quick judgment of the situation. Turning to Granny, he snapped his fingers in front of her face and with a feigned chuckle, he countered her words, "Snap out it, you crabby old woman! I thought I was the love of your life. You didn't kill him! Look at him, he's stiff. He's been dead for hours!"

"Crickett, can't you see she's upset? You don't belong here." Franklin pushed Silas away from Granny and towards the door.

Hearing Silas's words and seeing Franklin grabbing Silas, Granny stood up straight with a shrewd look in her eyes and quickly stepped between Silas and Franklin. Holding Franklin back and putting one hand on his chest, she turned to look Silas Crickett in the eye. "How do you know how long I've been here, Mr. Supercilious?"

Thor picked up the pitchfork and separated the three people before turning to his mother. "Mom, how did the blood get on this pitchfork?"

"I, uh, was testing it."

"By forking a dead body? And . . . why are you out here?" Thor's voice was agitated.

"Well," said Granny to her son, "I didn't know there was a dead body here, Thor. I was just testing this pitchfork for my new weapon."

Franklin threw his hands in the air. "You don't need a new weapon, Hermiony! We're getting married. You're retiring!"

Granny turned to Franklin with a furrowed brow, "What happened to 'I commit to accepting your colorful personality, your willful ways and your sparkling independence, Franklin?'" Turning to Thor, she asked, "Can I go now? I have somewhere I have to be."

Before Thor could answer, the rest of the police team pulled into the driveway.

"Granny, suppose we let everyone do their job and you meet us down at the police station," the Tall Guy suggested.

Franklin took Granny's arm. "I'll drive you there; you'll have to postpone wherever it is you have to be."

Granny moved her arm out of Franklin's clutches. "See that cute little red convertible! It's mine. I'm fine. I'm leaving the scene of the crime, Franklin. Alone! You go on home. The Police Station is well known. I can find my way there and what you do, well….I don't care. Granny has left the building!" With a brief nod, Granny quickly walked out the door.

Silas, a mischievous twinkle in his eye, turned to Franklin and sarcastically commented, "Didn't she just sparkle now?"

CHAPTER FIVE

Granny glanced at the clock in the Fuchsia Town Hall as she drove past the square on her way to the police station. It was 3:00 p.m. She would have to call Delight. They might not be able to meet in the underground street later. The surprise might have to wait. The other times she'd been questioned about dead bodies she'd found it hadn't taken too long. Of course, this might be the time they tried to break her down and make her confess to something she didn't do. She had seen those movies where they kept you for hours and didn't let you eat or sleep. Thor wouldn't do that to her, would he?

Instead of taking a right at the corner by Graves' Funeral Home to continue to the Police Station, Granny took a sharp left. Her car continued on past Racks Restaurant. She parked across the street in front of Esmeralda Periwinkle's old house. The house had been home to a few owners since Esmeralda had left this world, and the latest occupant was her twin sister, Amelia.

Before getting out of the car, Granny picked up her cell phone and shouted the word *coffee*. Granny could hear the phone ringing.

"We're perky, we're pink, and our sweets will make you wink," came the reply.

"Delight that was quite the poem," said Granny into the phone.

"Are you ready for our surprise, Granny?" Delight could be heard whispering to someone on the other end.

"We're going to have to postpone," said Granny.

"Postpone! It's your birthday. We can't postpone!" replied Delight.

"Would you like to tell that to the police?" Granny asked Delight.

"Police, police! What did you do now?" Delight's agitation vibrated through the connection.

"I didn't do anything. Just forked some hay. Do you suppose we could talk the prison officials into changing their prison garb to pink? I don't think I'll look good in orange," moaned Granny.

Before Delight could say another word, Granny hung up the phone and quickly got out of the car, glancing around to make sure the police weren't going to pounce on her, since she was here and not there— there being Police Headquarters.

Reaching back in the car, Granny grabbed her umbrella. You never knew when that hook would come in handy. Besides, she didn't know Amelia that well anymore. Maybe Amelia's meek demeanor was a cover.

Granny was ready to pound on the door with her umbrella when the door swung open. Amelia, not seeing Granny, walked straight into the umbrella. Granny's umbrella was on a downward swing for a knock, but instead of the umbrella hitting the door; it hit smack dab on top of Amelia's head.

As the umbrella came down on Amelia's head, a pink Fuchsia squad car parked behind Granny's car. The two men in the car, seeing what was happening, hurriedly exited the car.

"Stop! Mom, stop! What are you doing?" Thor shouted.

The Tall Guy was quicker and made it up the steps just as Amelia was falling. Amelia fell into Granny and

Granny fell backwards straight into the arms of the Tall Guy.

Granny looked up at the Tall Guy as he caught her, "You know what happened the last time I fell for someone?" Granny asked innocently, referring to the fact that she'd met Franklin by falling into his arms.

Thor, finally getting to the fracas, helped Amelia back onto her feet. Turning to his mother, he gave her a look of exasperation. "First, we find you with a dead body and now we find you assaulting your sister. And—you failed to obey our instructions. You're supposed to be at the police station!"

"Now I'll have to arrest you!" The Tall Guy stood Granny up, out of his arms.

"No, no! It wasn't like that!" a rattled Amelia tried to explain. "I was coming out of the house just as she was knocking at my door with her umbrella. Dead body? What dead body? Hermiony?"

Granny stood up straight and shook off the Tall Guy's hand which was holding her arm. "That's why I'm here, Amelia. You didn't think I'd visit ya unless I had a good reason. Your husband's dead. Did you kill him?"

At the word *husband* and *dead*, Amelia's entire body visibly shook. "Where? What? What are you talking about?"

Thor stood in front of his aunt. "I know this is a shock, Aunt Amelia, but that's why we're here. We just got the id on the body and it was—"

"Robert Blackford!" said Granny, "the love of my life! Amelia stole him from me! And she's probably the one who killed him!" Granny pointed a finger at her sister.

"Let's all go inside and sit down," the Tall Guy suggested, again taking Granny's arm and moving past

Thor and Amelia into the house. An agitated Amelia let Thor lead her in after them.

After they were seated, the Tall Guy continued for Thor. "We got the id on the person you forked in the hay mound, Granny. His name is Dickey Lee Hatchet. We found his wallet on his body."

"I don't know where you got that name," Granny said, expressing her disbelief, "but his name is Robert Blackford. Do you think I'd forget what the love of my life looked like?"

Granny turned to Amelia. "What did you do to him?"

Thor broke in, "And he escaped from prison about six months ago. The reason we came here, was because he had a picture of Amelia in his pocket. Do either of you know why he was here?"

"Hermiony," said the Tall Guy, "since this Dickey Lee Hatchet was found on your farm, perhaps you were hiding him because he looked like this Robert Blackford you claim is the love of your life."

"In case you forgot," replied Granny, incensed, "six months ago, I was busy planning my wedding and snowing a sneak. You think I had time to play hide and seek too with Robert—and that's who that dead man is, Robert Blackford, not Dickey Lee Hatchet or Cratchet or whoever you claim he is."

Amelia cleared her throat and timidly suggested, "Well, um, um, you didn't marry Franklin, Hermiony, and you haven't set another wedding date. Maybe this Robert look-alike was the reason." Amelia cleared her throat again and in a low voice said, "There's something none of you but Hermiony knows. I was married to Robert Blackford. He left, out of the blue, when I was 20 years old and we'd only been married a couple of years. He took our son with him. I haven't seen either of them since. I came back to Fuchsia on the chance that he might have come back here. I want to find my son. All the detectives I hired over the years couldn't locate either one of them. Now, however, I am more hopeful because of all the new developments in forensic science."

"You have a son?" Granny asked Amelia. Then she turned to Thor and the Tall Guy, "That dead man is Robert Blackford!" Turning back to her sister, Granny paused before speaking, "Well, Amelia, you're not off the hook yet for stealing Robert from me, but if I have a nephew, I'm going to help you find him."

Turning once again to look at the two men, Granny continued, "And I didn't kill him! But it's a good thing he's dead or I would kill him! I'd fork him with that pitchfork! But you really need to change those orange jumpsuits you use in the hoosegow to pink. It's a better color for me. You know, just in case I ever need one."

CHAPTER SIX

It was after six by the time Granny got back to her house. Despite her protests, Thor and the Tall Guy followed her to the police station to be questioned about her part in finding the body at her old farm. They wanted details and they wouldn't question her in front of Amelia—something about the two sisters possibly being in cahoots with each other. What a birthday this had turned out to be!

Granny looked around the room to see if any of the shysters or their cohorts were home. All appeared to be silent. They probably were out on their run of the town before ending up at Franklin's house. Their routine still wasn't back to normal since the last murder investigation had been solved. Granny called Fish, Little White Poodle, Furball and Tank her shysters because she'd acquired them during Gram Gramstead's crime spree and, without their help, Granny wouldn't have solved the crime. Of course, Furball and Tank were Franklin's, aka Itsy and Bitsy. Granny had renamed them to more fit their character. Add that to the fact that they were always in trouble, and the name *shyster* fit perfectly. Baskerville and Mrs. Bleaty didn't quite seem like shysters though, so Granny decided to call them cohorts, because they were always right in the thick of things too.

The creatures' usual routine had been to show up at Granny's house around four in the afternoon, leave around 10:00 p.m., check out the town, and head to Franklin's house around 5:00 a.m. They'd stay there until 10:00 or 11:00 a.m. before they headed out again to patrol the town. It had been a daily routine until Silas Crickett moved in across the street with his loud-mouthed Radish—a gray parrot. Baskerville fell in love with the parrot, and Silas used this relationship to woo Granny's pets to his house where he had a pet play room in his basement. She and Franklin now had a hard time keeping the shysters and the cohorts out of trouble, and out of Silas's house.

Reaching down to take the top off her footstool, Granny moved the false insides around and took out her wine and a glass. It was her birthday, after all. She didn't know why she still bothered to hide her wine in the footstool. It was becoming common knowledge to all of her friends and family that Granny imbibed occasionally, and that she hid her wine in the footstool. Maybe she'd move it soon. *A false wall*, she thought, *maybe a false wall somewhere they wouldn't suspect.* Granny poured herself a glass of wine and sat down to survey the room, looking for the perfect place for a false wall.

While drinking her wine, thoughts of the dead body--Robert Blackford—swirled around in her head. Why was he at the farm? How long had he been there? And why now, just when Amelia had come back? Granny set the wine glass down on the table next to her chair and closed her eyes, remembering her eighteenth birthday.

A loud pounding coming from somewhere in the basement woke Granny up. She must have fallen asleep while reminiscing about her eighteenth birthday. With a frown on her face, she lifted her cell phone to her eyes to check out the time. It was midnight! The pounding got louder!

Granny grabbed her umbrella which was sitting beside the front door, and for good measure, added her knitting needle cane—her two favorite weapons—before descending the steps into her basement and family room to see what or who was pounding. Where were the shysters when you needed them?

The noise seemed to be coming from the other side of the hidden fireplace door. Someone was pounding on the door to the underground streets. Granny reached into the fireplace and pushed the latch to open the secret door that wasn't so secret anymore, switching on the light and moving through the room to the outer door.

"Stop! I've got weapons! Go away or I'm going to let my guard dog out!" Granny yelled. *Where was Baskerville when she needed him?*

"Granny! Granny! It's us—Delight and Mavis. Open the door!"

"It's midnight. How do I know it's really you?" Granny countered.

"Boneyard!" Delight shouted.

Granny opened the door because Boneyard specialty coffee was Granny's favorite coffee.

"What are you doing here?" she asked the two women. "It's midnight!"

"It's time for our surprise! Come on," Mavis urged.

"Did you really fork someone at your farm? We didn't know you still owned the farm," Delight questioned, while taking Granny's arm. Mavis took the umbrella and knitting needle cane out of Granny's hands and laid them down inside the room, before taking Granny's other arm and leading her into the lighted underground street.

"Where are we going? It's past my bedtime!" Granny tried to change the subject.

Delight giggled, "It's a surprise! You'll see."

The streets were pretty much deserted this time of night. The residents of Fuchsia didn't use the underground streets as much during the summer as they did in the winter, except when it was raining. The underground also made a good tornado shelter when the weather was bad.

When they reached Graves' Funeral Home, Granny stopped. "Now what? The underground street ends here."

Mavis, ever the dramatic one, gestured wildly with her arms. "After you, my dear! Your carriage awaits you."

Granny skewered up her face, lifted her eyebrows and said, "In case you haven't noticed, I'm not Cinderella and you'd better not have a fella waiting for me at whatever carriage you're talking about. I've had enough of fellas for the day, and I don't see any carriage anyway."

"Granny, use your imagination. Get with the program," Mavis instructed, miffed that Granny wasn't playing along with her make-believe show.

Delight giggled again. "Never mind, Mavis. Granny, the new street is open to the Pink Percolator. We're going to have a midnight party! Come on." Delight moved to Granny's right and Mavis moved to Granny's left, each taking one arm to escort her down the new underground street and up the stairs to the Pink Percolator.

When they got to the top of the stairs and Delight opened the door to the Pink Percolator, it was dark. Mavis gave Granny a little push to get her into the shop. As Granny stepped through the door, the lights came on and Granny felt something light and stringy touching her body, at the same time she heard the word *surprise* echoed over and over again.

Looking up, Granny saw Lulu from the quilt shop, Ditty Belle, and a woman she didn't recognize squirting pink wacky string right at her. On the counter was a cake that looked just like Granny with a knitting needle as a candle in the Granny cake's hand.

Extricating herself from the wacky string, Granny's eyes misted over a little and she said, "I'm old, you're bold, but this is gold!"

Lulu led her over to one of the chairs. "Sit here while we get you some cake and a little wine."

Delight was already pouring the wine as Mavis was cutting the cake.

They all scooted their chairs into a circle around the table and then lifted their glasses in a toast to Granny.

"She likes wine, she has a mind, of her own and she has a clone!" Mavis raised her glass to clink it together with the others.

"She's ornery, she's old, but to us, she's our pot of gold!" Delight rhymed, raising her glass for another clink with the ladies."

"She doesn't knit, when she's in a snit, she purls and whirls to make her point and make someone oink!" The glasses clinked as Lulu finished her rhyme.

"Oink?" Granny questioned, taking an extra sip.

"She reads with the best, but it's her zest that cleans up the mest!"

Granny turned toward Ditty Belle before clinking her glass with the others, "Mest?"

Ditty Belle lifted her eyebrows and gave Granny a haughty look. "Yes, *mest*. I made the word up in honor of your birthday."

Granny turned to the woman they'd invited to the party she didn't know. "Who are you and why are you here?"

"Granny, you're a legend and when I overheard them whispering they were going to have this surprise party for you tonight, I asked if I could attend. Can I have your autograph? You're a legend at the *We Save You Christian Church.*"

Granny gave the woman a skeptical look before turning with a questioning look to Mavis and Delight.

Delight giggled. "Granny, this is the new pastor at We Save You Christian Church. She took Pastor Snicks' place. She just arrived this past week and we became acquainted. Meet Pastor Henrietta Romans."

"You're a pastor?" asked Granny and then turned to the others, "You invited a pastor to my birthday? You invited a pastor to my birthday and you're plying her with wine? And you didn't warn me? Franklin isn't hidden around here somewhere, is he?" Granny looked around suspiciously. "You're not planning a surprise wedding too, are you?" She stood up ready to leave. "I'm not quite ready for that yet," she warned them, sprinting toward the door.

Mavis and Delight caught up with her right before she made it out the door. "Relax, she's one of us. We're going to help you solve this new crime. No one will suspect Pastor Henrietta is one of us," Mavis informed Granny.

Lulu nodded her head in agreement. "Yes, and Ditty Belle and I want in on the excitement too!"

"And what better person to have on our team than a pastor; they hear everything!" Delight added.

"Well, I can't divulge everything," Henrietta warned them and then giggled. "But I can help. I'm an expert." Motioning them closer, she continued in a conspiratorial voice, "You see, I read mysteries. And at my last church, I figured out who stole the communion wine and hid it in the base of the baptismal font. And then, I planted seeds of suspicion in my sermon to get the crook to make a mistake and give himself away. And he did! So, I know I can help you, Granny."

"Mavis retreated into the Pink Percolator kitchen and returned with a tall, long, wrapped present in her arms.

This is for you, Granny. We got it this afternoon after we heard the news."

"We had a hard time knowing what to get you and then we heard the news about the body you found and we just knew!" Delight announced, a proud smile on her face, taking the present from Mavis and presenting it to Granny.

Granny unwrapped the present.

"Careful, you might get forked," smirked Ditty Belle.

Granny lifted her present—a bright, pink-handled, fuchsia-colored pitchfork. "You gave me a pitchfork because I forked a dead body that turned out to be my long-lost love Robert Blackford?"

Mavis moved forward and looked Granny straight in the face. "It's the perfect weapon to protect you and us while we snoop out the scene of the crime."

Granny gave them a perplexed look.

The women surrounded Granny. "Tell us what you know," Lulu commanded.

"I forked Robert Blackford."

"You never told us you still owned that farm," Mavis scolded.

"Why were you there in the first place?" Ditty Belle asked.

Henrietta took Granny's arm and led her back to the table and motioned for her to sit down in the chair. The others followed and sat down too. Henrietta reached across the table and put her hand on Granny's arm, assumed her most sympathetic look, and said in her most pastor-like tone, "Now, Granny, you said that you forked the love of your life. How hard that must have been for you. I think you need to talk about it. It will be better for you to talk to someone about this instead of keeping it all bottled up inside."

Granny pulled her arm away from Henrietta and looked at the other women. "Okay, she's in. She's got a good interrogation technique."

At her acceptance into the group, Henrietta said to Granny, "Spill it, Granny."

Granny told the women about her experience at the farm, about her interrogation at the police station, and her sister's involvement in the case.

Mavis looked at the clock on the wall "It's time to go."

"Go where? Home? Yes, I am kind of tired," sighed Granny.

"You're getting old, Granny," Delight chided, "But this party isn't ended. Grab your new pitchfork!"

Ditty Belle cut the lights. "We'll go out the back door. I brought my van. We can all get in that." Ditty Belle ushered them over to the waiting vehicle.

"Stop!" Granny said in a loud voice.

"Shh!" the other women all said at once.

"We don't want anyone to hear us," Lulu warned.

"I'm not going anywhere until you tell me what you have planned. Are we hunting zombies in the cemetery?"

"No, we're going back to investigate the scene of the crime," Mavis informed Granny, hustling her into the van. The van slowly moved through the dark streets of Fuchsia—they thought, unseen.

CHAPTER SEVEN

All was quiet when the van carrying Granny and her friends pulled into the old abandoned farm yard. The night was dark, and clouds overhead kept the stars from lighting the night sky.

Granny was the first out of the van. Mavis handed Granny the pitchfork and passed out the flashlights that she'd thrown in the van when the women had hatched the plan to celebrate Granny's birthday doing what Granny loved best—sleuthing.

Shining her flashlight toward the silo, Granny could see that the crime scene tape was gone and the scene had been cleaned up. She turned to her friends who now seemed to be a little more uncertain that this was the right thing to do.

"Did you hear that?" Ditty Belle whispered, moving closer to Lulu.

"Something just touched my leg," Lulu answered as she grabbed Ditty Belle.

"It's Ditty Belle's leg; want me to fork it to prove it to you?" Granny's crusty attitude was revealing itself again.

Mavis, panicking, asked, "Did you see that? Did you see that?"

"What?" Granny rasped.

"Something moved in what is left of the house in the upstairs window!" cried Lulu.

Granny glanced up at the window and moved her flashlight beam in the same direction. "Relax, it's just a bat."

"A bat, a bat, it's a bat! It's going to get in my hair. It's going to bite me!" Lulu ran around in a circle swatting over her head and moving towards the van.

Henrietta grabbed Lulu's arm and, in a quiet, soothing tone said, "Lulu, my dear. God will protect you. He sent that bat to eat the mouse that's by your feet."

"Henrietta, I mean, Pastor Henrietta, I think you and I are going to get along fine!" Laughing, Granny moved towards Lulu. "She's kidding, Lulu. No rat, no bat. It was just an old curtain blowing in the wind."

"What should we look for?" Ditty Belle asked.

"Anything that would explain Robert Blackford's presence here at the farm," said Granny.

"I thought they said his name was Dickey Lee Hatchet. I know you think it's this Robert Blackford, but your friends think it's this Dickey Lee," Henrietta countered, "At least that was what I heard when Franklin, your fiancé, and Silas, your neighbor, were visiting your sister late this afternoon."

Granny frowned. "Visiting my sister? They were visiting Amelia? How did you know that? I didn't know that."

"I was making a visit to see if she'd like to join We Save You Christian Church. They were just wrapping up their visit when I got there," replied Henrietta.

"Hmm, I wondered why they didn't follow me to the Police Station," mused Granny. "It seemed too quiet on that front. Are you sure they were together? Last I saw them, they didn't like each other too much."

"I didn't hear much," replied Henrietta. "They both had glowering looks on their faces when they came in. Then when that Franklin of yours saw your sister, he had a smile so wide it might have cracked his face. The other guy, the one you call Mr. Supercilious—Mavis told me that—kept on glowering and then they ushered me to the door. Like they couldn't trust a pastor? I was miffed."

"Did you hear that?" Lulu asked, hearing a noise through the darkness, and she moved closer to Granny.

"I heard it," Ditty Belle said, and hid behind Granny. "Well, she has the weapon!" said Ditty Belle, explaining why she hid behind Granny.

"Don't they usually have yard lights out here?" Mavis tapped the post that should have had the light.

"There's nothing here but a broken old house and a silo. Why would I waste good electricity on yard lights?" Granny shook her head, "I don't hear anything; relax. Mavis and I'll take a good look inside and around the silo. Ditty Belle, Lulu, Delight, and Pastor Henrietta, you all take a look around the grounds and the outside of the house."

"Um, maybe I should go with them, Granny," Mavis suggested in a hushed voice. "There's safety in numbers."

Granny skewered her with a look. "Mavis, just pretend we're in *The Farmer in the Dell* reality show. We're looking for the cheese, or the rat. Come on. Let's go!"

The others fanned out around the house, staying close to one another. Only Ditty Belle was brave enough to break off from the other three and head toward the back of the house.

Granny and Mavis continued on to the silo. Once inside the silo, Granny and Mavis examined the cement floor, inch by inch using their flashlight to show them the way. It appeared that all evidence had been swept away and the floor was clean. The hay had been removed.

Granny was about to study a pencil marking that appeared to be written on the bottom edge of the cement wall when a scream broke through the quiet night.

"Help! Help me! He's got me; he's got me!" Ditty Belle screamed into the night.

Granny ran through the door of the silo into the dark night toward the sound of the screams, pitchfork out in front of her. Mavis picked up a loose rock she'd tripped on while exiting the silo, raising her arm ready to throw when she could see her target.

"Let me go! Let me go! I didn't see anything!" Ditty Belle pleaded with her captor.

Granny and Mavis met up with the other women just as they were rounding the corner of the house.

"It's Ditty Belle! He's got her," Lulu stated.

"Who's got her?" Granny asked as she shushed everyone trying to hear where the screams were coming from. "I thought Ditty Belle was with you."

"She decided to check out the back of the house by herself," Pastor Henrietta added.

Just then, Ditty Belle let out another screech, "Ouch! You're hurting me; let me go. Help! He's going to kill me!"

"Okay; she's in the back. Turn the flashlights off. We'll sneak up. When I give the count, everyone turn on your flashlights at once. We'll blind him and I'll fork him. Pastor Henrietta, you get ready to grab Ditty Belle. Delight, have your cell phone ready to dial the police. Let's go," Granny instructed.

Quietly, holding on to each other in the dark, they moved towards the back of the house. Ditty Belle was no longer screaming, but making little whimpering sounds.

"She's dying," Lulu whispered, "We're too late."

Ready to go around the corner to the back of the house, Granny started her count down, "One, two, and three!"

At the count of three, Granny sprang out from the side of the house, pitchfork poised to attack. All flashlights flicked on and aimed at the sounds coming from the direction of Ditty Belle.

Seeing Ditty Belle, Granny let out a loud laugh and lowered her pitchfork to the ground. The other women, seeing what the beam of their flashlights revealed, chuckled, and soon were bellowing with laughter.

"What's so funny? Kill him, he's got me!" Ditty Belle pleaded.

"Yes, he certainly does," Granny answered, still chuckling. Moving forward, she moved to Ditty Belle and began untangling her from the brambles of the big bush that held her captive. "You've been captured by Mr. Barney Bramble, as we used to call this bush when we were kids, although he certainly has gotten a lot bigger since then."

The other women moved forward. Pastor Henrietta held the flashlight while the women untangled Ditty Belles' clothes from the bush.

"How did you get caught, Ditty Belle?" Mavis asked, trying to distract her as she pulled a prickly branch out of Ditty Belle's hair.

"I heard a noise. It sounded like someone pounding on a door in the back of the house. But when I got back here, there was no door, just all of these trees and bushes. I turned around to call to all of you, when it got me! Are you sure you didn't all scare away whoever was holding me? It felt like arms encircling my neck."

Granny dangled a vine in front of Ditty's face. "These are the arms of the culprit. Somehow when you turned around you stepped backwards right into this bush and the vines."

"What about the noise? Someone was knocking."

Pastor Henrietta gave Ditty a disbelieving look. "My dear, Ditty," she said in a soothing tone, "I'm sure with your exquisite hearing and your anxiety about the darkness, your ears perhaps were hearing God's knock on your heart."

"Or your head," Granny interjected.

"There aren't even any doors back here. All that are here are bushes and—look!" Mavis pointed out, shining her flashlight at the base of the house, "There isn't even a basement."

Granny picked a last twig off Ditty Belle and directed her flashlight beam into the thickness of the bushes. "That's it! There *is* a basement. It used to be one of those stone basements, but Ferdinand wanted a bomb shelter and a basement that no one would know was there; he always said, 'You can't be too careful. You never know when you might have to hide from the bill collectors.' He had the house lifted up, built a concrete basement and a slab, and put the house down on top of it. It's even with the ground and has no windows and no access from the inside. You don't even know it's there. Maybe that's where Robert Blackford was hiding."

Delight shone her flashlight on the bushes and thick undergrowth. "It doesn't look like anyone has bothered it in a long time."

"Shush; hear that?" Ditty Belle whispered. "I told you I heard knocking."

A thumping could be heard from deep in the brush.

Granny moved to the corner of the house, next to the side, and directed her flashlight beam on the ground. Reaching down, she tentatively touched the branches of the bushes that were on the ground. "They're loose. We used to have a path right here behind these bushes that no one could see." She grabbed the big branch of the bush and moved it aside. The others followed behind Granny, shining their flashlights to light the path as

Granny used the pitchfork to move the brush away. Finally, she reached a spot near the middle of the house.

They could hear thumping continuing underneath their feet. "Something's buried alive!" Ditty Belle exclaimed.

Granny held up her hand and put a finger to her mouth to gesture the others to be quiet as she whispered, "Something's in the basement. There's a door under this last piece of brush. Someone covered it up good. Move the brush and open the door. I'll be ready with my pitchfork. On the count of three! One....two...three!"

Mavis lifted up the last piece of brush. Pastor Henrietta pulled up the door. Ditty hid behind Granny and the pitchfork. Granny lifted her pitchfork ready to strike when a medium-sized squiggly creature made a loud oink and bounded up and out of the basement steps and outside, past the women, into the darkness.

"You missed it!" Mavis yelled at Granny.

"It was a pig! I couldn't fork a pork!" cried Granny.

"What was a pig doing in your basement?" Pastor Henrietta asked Granny.

"How am I to know? Remember yesterday was the first time I've been back here since Ferdinand died. Maybe porky the pig left his ghost in my basement and he wanted a pastor to put him out to pasture," Granny answered sarcastically.

"Granny, you can't talk about a pastor like that," Mavis admonished Granny.

Granny ignored Mavis, flashed the beam of light from her flashlight into the darkness before moving down the basement steps, her pitchfork poised in front of her. "Let's see what other secrets my old basement holds."

"Maybe we should call Thor and the Tall Guy," Delight suggested.

"This is my birthday. Remember, this is my party. Come on, let's get the party started." Granny led the way into the dark basement.

They all congregated down at the bottom of the steps in a huddle.

"Now what?" Pastor Henrietta whispered, moving into the darkness of the basement, illuminating the walls with the light from her flashlight. The others did the same.

The beam from Granny's flashlight landed on a camping lantern. She moved to the lantern and turned the switch. It lit up the darkness, revealing a cozy room that had been set up. Food sat on the table in the corner. "I guess we were right; Robert Blackford must have been living here."

"With a porker," Mavis answered.

"But why? Why would he have come back here and why live in secret? Why live on *your* abandoned farm, Granny? How did he know there even was a basement? And who else knew? Maybe the murderer is still here?" Ditty Belle rattled off questions without waiting for answers until she asked the last question and realized what she'd just said. Then, she shuffled over close to Granny, grabbing Granny's arm to hold the pitchfork in front of them both.

"Look! There's another room." Lulu, who'd been silent since Ditty Belle's capture by Mr. Bramble, shone the beam of her flashlight onto another door off to the left of where the women were standing.

"That used to be a bedroom. We had one down here in case it stormed and we had to spend the night. Someone really cleaned this place up," said Granny, moving around the room, noticing the clean surfaces. "But they must not have taken out the trash because it's kind of smelly down here."

Lulu wandered over to the door and poked her head into the old bedroom while shining her flashlight over the shapes in the dark room. She let out a scream, dropped her flashlight and ran back over and hid behind Granny.

"Now what's wrong? Let's get this straight, Lulu, if you're going to sleuth with me you're going to have to get over this screaming at every shadow," Granny instructed the women.

"Ah, ah, ah, but...but...but someone's sleeping in the bed," Lulu stammered.

Granny grabbed Lulu's hand to loosen the grip she'd placed on Granny as she was trying to explain what she'd seen. "If they were sleeping, they won't be now," Granny rasped, "That scream was enough to wake the dead." Granny grabbed the camping lantern and held tight to her pitchfork before moving towards the door of the old bedroom.

The others, not wanting to be left alone and wanting to see what Lulu had found, moved together in a tightly knit group towards the door.

Entering the room, Granny approached what appeared to be a lump under the covers on the bed.

"Lulu, it's probably just a lump of blankets. Robert Blackford surely didn't bother to make the bed the morning he was offed by the haystack killer," Granny surmised as she pulled back the covers.

Ditty Belle, Lulu, and Mavis gasped and jumped back away from the bed and Granny. Pastor Henrietta moved forward for a closer look before reaching out her hand and closing the eyes of the still man in the bed. She said a quick prayer and turned to Granny, "Do you know him?"

Granny shook her head, "Never saw him before in my life; looks like someone got him with a knife."

CHAPTER EIGHT

The sound of something padding down the steps of the old basement silenced whatever Granny had been going to say to finish her statement.

"Someone's coming!" Mavis warned.

"It could be the killer!" Ditty Belle said in alarm.

"Let's not panic," Pastor Henrietta whispered, "the Lord will protect us, but just in case, everyone get into the corner over here." Henrietta moved quickly to be first in the corner of the room.

"Shut your flashlights off; they'll see us," Granny instructed, killing the light from her lantern and getting her pitchfork ready. "We'll surprise them. When I move with the fork, you all start screaming to distract them."

"No problem," said Delight.

The women huddled together silently in the dark corner with Granny in front of them, pitchfork raised. The darkness was thick so no movement could be seen. They heard the tick, tick, on the cement floor telling them the intruder was getting closer. They saw no movement.

Delight reached out to touch Mavis. Mavis put her hand on Granny's shoulder. Henrietta moved over closer to Ditty Belle as Ditty Belle hugged her in response. Lulu stood shivering, silently, trying to melt back into the cement of the wall.

Ahhwoo! Ahhwoo! A howl split the darkness and silence of the room. The women all screamed as flashlights hit their faces.

"Baskerville, enough!" Granny commanded, putting down her pitchfork.

"Dagnabit, woman! What kind of trouble are you in now?" Silas Crickett's voice came out of the darkness.

"You trying to blind me, Silas?" Granny countered, looking into the bright lights that were shining into their faces.

"Mavis, you told me you were going to Granny's party at the Pink Percolator."

"George," Mavis's quivery voice questioned, "is that you?" Getting over her fear and realizing that George wasn't supposed to be here, she moved forward. "You followed me. And this is Granny's birthday party."

"What are you doing here, Mr. Supercilious?" Granny asked Silas, momentarily forgetting about the dead body in the bed behind her.

"When George told me there was a birthday party at midnight with a bunch of old ladies," replied Silas, "I knew you had something planned. I told George we'd better check it out and join the party."

"And Baskerville?" Granny touched Baskerville's head as he moved behind Granny to sniff at the aroma that was originating from the bed. He let out a blood curdling howl.

"We watched you leave," continued Silas. "I figured we'd find you here since Thor told you not to come here. We parked up the road and walked. By the time we got here, you'd disappeared. Hence, we put Baskerville to work," he added sarcastically. "We brought him along just in case we needed to look for your body."

George covered his ears as Baskerville let out another yowl. "What's he yowling about?"

"Um," Granny hesitated.

"The dead body, the dead body!" Mavis blurted out.

"Dead body?" Silas brushed past Granny, shining his flashlight on the bed, revealing the dead body. "By the smell of things, he's dead alright. I noticed the smell when we first came down the stairs but then you screamers distracted me. We'd better call my son, Ephraim, and Thor. How did you know he was down here? And why didn't the police find this basement and this body when they were investigating the one in the silo?"

"We didn't know a body was here. We were just having fun for my birthday party," said Granny. "You don't think women our age can have fun?" Granny poked Silas in the chest with her finger to make her point. "We were zombie hunting!"

"Yah, zombie hunting!" Mavis backed up Granny's statement by also nodding her head.

Delight giggled. "Didn't you ever go zombie hunting in the dark out in the country? Although, the last time I went zombie hunting I was teenager and I had a big strong guy to protect me."

"We were recreating our youth," Ditty Belle said with a challenging tone in her voice.

"Well, you found your zombie," said Silas. "I'm going above ground to call Ephraim. George, be a strong arm for these zombie hunters to hold on to as you escort them out of the basement to wait for the police."

Silas was finishing his phone call when the zombie hunters and George ascended from the basement and made their way through the prickly bramble path back to the side of the house, joining him. Turning to Granny, he looked at her and shook his head. "Granny, to say your son and my son are upset with you might be understating the problem you're going to have when they get here."

"And you got Mavis into this!" George huffed.

"George!" cried Mavis, "It was my idea. This will be a great script for our reality show."

"And ours too. Don't blame Granny. All for one and one for all!" Ditty Belle stated.

"Yah!" the others chimed in, closing rank around Granny.

Her pitch fork hit the ground with a thud as Granny lifted it up high and then forked the dirt making the pitchfork stand straight up on its own. "We've got to get our story straight," she said.

"And what story might that be?" Silas asked, "Zombie hunting? forking a fragile body? Leading these women into trouble? Or forgetting you're old and supposed to be home and in bed?" The tone of his voice got louder as his questions continued.

Granny was spared from answering as the police cars with their loud sirens turned into the driveway.

"Was that necessary?" Granny quipped when Thor and the Tall Guy came within hearing distance of the group. "You'll wake the dead. Of course, if we woke the dead, he could tell us who he was."

"Hermiony Vidalia Fiddlestadt, you are going to have to explain yourself," Franklin admonished, appearing out of the darkness behind Thor and the Tall Guy.

Scowling at Franklin, Granny said, "What are you doing here, Franklin? Can't a woman celebrate her birthday with a few girl friends in peace without her fiancé following her? Shouldn't you be in bed?"

"I called him," Thor told his mother, "After what Silas told me, I thought we could use his detective expertise and his expertise with you."

The Tall Guy broke into the conversation, speaking to Silas, "Suppose you show us where this body is. Franklin, keep an eye on this crowd of zombie hunters."

"Why don't all of you go and sit in your van while they take a look at what you found," Franklin suggested. Then, taking Granny's arm, he said, "I'll take the keys first and I'll take Granny to my car."

After confiscating the keys from the van and seeing that the women and George were comfortably settled, Franklin led Granny back to his car. He handed her a cup of coffee from a thermos that was in the vehicle. "I just happened to have made a new pot of coffee and was going to have a cup when Thor called. I couldn't sleep thinking about the events of the day."

Granny took the cup of coffee. "You aren't going to ask what I was doing out here?"

Franklin sighed, "No, you drive me crazy. First there's a sister you don't tell me about and then there's a farm you don't tell me about. Then there's a dead body on your farm you claim is the love of your life—someone I've never heard of. What could top that?" He poured himself a cup of coffee, held the cup up to Granny's cup and toasted, "To the many surprises of Hermiony Vidalia Criony Fiddlestadt, soon to be Hermiony Vidalia Criony Fiddlestadt Gatsby. May I survive them!"

They sipped in silence waiting to see movement to announce that Silas, Thor, and the Tall Guy were out of the basement. Soon, more police cars and a van pulled into the driveway. The occupants of the vehicles got out and headed toward the falling down house. Another fifteen minutes passed before they saw Thor and the Tall Guy headed their way.

Granny scrambled out of the car. "So do you know who it is?"

"The wallet we found under the body indicated that it's Robert Blackford." Thor watched the face of his mother closely.

"Robert Blackford! That's not Robert Blackford. Robert Blackford is the man I found yesterday. I mean it was yesterday, isn't it? It's after midnight. I've never seen this new dead guy before in my life."

"We'll get into that later," the Tall Guy said. "We need you all to come down to the police station. We'll follow you this time." The Tall Guy then instructed Franklin, "You take Granny and don't let her out of your sight." Turning to Silas who'd just walked up behind them, he said, "You'll need to come down too, Dad."

"You need to find out why he was here," Granny piped up, pointing at Silas. "He wasn't invited."

"Why, Hermiony," Silas said, smiling sweetly, "I'd follow you anywhere."

Franklin glared at Silas, took Granny's arm and led her back to his car. Opening the car door for Granny and settling her into the front seat, he muttered to himself as he moved around the car to the driver's side, "Silas needs to go back to Alaska. There must be a serial killer somewhere who's missing him."

CHAPTER NINE

"Is it necessary to put us all in a different room?" Granny questioned as Franklin led her to Thor's office. "We could at least chat while we were waiting."

"Hermiony, you should know the drill by now. You've been here enough times. They want to make sure all your stories match."

"Didn't you know matching is not the style anymore, Franklin?" Granny batted her eyes at Franklin, trying to distract him.

"Hermiony, all this has to stop! You can't keep putting yourself in danger—and you won't once we're married."

At the words, *you won't*, Granny's back stiffened. Just as she was about to reply, a young policeman entered the room. "Do you know what time it is, young man? I should have been in bed hours ago. I demand to speak to your superior."

"Uh, I'm just here to offer you some coffee."

"You want to ply me with drink so I'll talk, don't you?" Granny used her most threatening voice.

"Uh, ah, would you like some coffee, ma'am?"

"No, I want my lawyer!"

"Uh, um, ok. I'll tell the chief." The young policeman backed out of the room.

Granny turned to Franklin, "I want my lawyer."

"You don't have a lawyer."

"I don't? I should. There have been enough times they've harassed me—my own son too! I need to get one. Maybe Silas knows a good lawyer." Granny eyed Franklin with a wicked grin.

"If you need a lawyer, Granny, I'll get you one," Franklin declared.

Granny walked over to the window that opened into the station and peered out. "Why aren't they questioning me so I can go home? They appear to be talking to everyone else first. Do you suppose they're listening to what we're saying so I'll incriminate myself?"

Franklin shook his head and a loud bellowing laugh shook the room.

"What are you laughing at, Franklin Jester Gatsby? Are you laughing at a scared old woman?"

"No, I'm laughing because life with you is never dull, just like it was with my momma. She drove me crazy. You drive me crazy, but you keep it exciting. I've got to admit that. Now, sit down until they get here to question you. Why don't you take a nap in the chair?"

"After all that coffee you fed me out on the farm? You plied me with coffee so I'd stay awake and now you want me to sleep? I can see why New York retired you." Granny paced back and forth.

The door finally opened and the Tall Guy entered the room. "Okay, Granny, it's your turn. Why don't you tell me what happened."

"What's there to tell? The bump turned out to be a lump. I thought it was a joke, so I gave him a poke. He was cold, but not too old."

Franklin threw his hands up in the air and walked out of the room.

"Something I said?" Granny innocently asked the Tall Guy.

"I'm going to let you off the hook this time, Granny. Everyone's story matches—except yours. However, since you were with the others, I will overlook your little story."

"Can I go now? A girl needs her beauty sleep, you know. Besides, it's my birthday! Do you know how old I am?"

"How old are you?"

Granny looked at the Tall Guy with disbelief. "You have the *nerve* to ask a girl's age? Didn't that Mr. Supercilious father of yours teach you any manners?"

The door opened and Thor, Franklin, and the others came into the room.

"Are we continuing the party?" Granny asked sarcastically.

"We now know who the victims are. We ran their fingerprints," Thor continued. "The first body you found was, indeed, Robert Blackford. The second body you found was Dickey Lee Hatchet."

"I told you that the first one was the love of my life, Robert Blackford. Did you arrest my sister? Did she do it?"

"Why would you think Aunt Amelia killed these two men, Mom?" asked Thor.

"She was the last person I saw with Robert Blackford all those years ago. She stole Robert Blackford from me. So who's to say she wasn't the last person to see him now. After all, why would they both show up in Fuchsia after all these years? Tell them, Pastor Henrietta. I know you're in cahoots with Franklin and Silas. Tell them what you saw when you were there?"

Pastor Henrietta's eyes widened as she looked at all the expectant faces in the room. Silas's face had a mischievous grin on his face, while Franklin's had a look of guilt. "Now, Hermiony," Pastor Henrietta patted Granny's hand as she took it between her two hands. "I know you're upset, but Franklin and Silas were just helping a poor, sweet, innocent old woman. Amelia's your sister. Why, when I left, she was crying in Franklin's arms. My dear Hermiony, let's take a breath and meditate on this." Pastor Henrietta looked Granny straight in the eyes and winked. Turning to the others, she said, "I think Granny has had enough for one night. She just found out that the love of her life died. What a birthday surprise! Let me take her home and pray with her."

Granny gave Pastor Henrietta a skeptical look, then said, "Yes, I need to go home. Pastor Henrietta is just what I need right now." Granny gave a fake little sob.

As Pastor Henrietta led Granny from the room, Mavis piped up, "Happy Birthday, Granny!" She turned around and gestured for everyone to follow her lead.

"Happy Birthday, Granny!" rang out through the room. Only Silas was silent. He would wish Granny a Happy Birthday later. He was sure she'd want to hear what he had to say.

CHAPTER TEN

The sun was coming up on the horizon when Pastor Henrietta dropped Granny off at her house. "Get some sleep, Granny. We'll see you in church on Sunday. Thanks for sharing your birthday with a stranger. If all your birthdays are like this, I'm in."

Granny waved Pastor Henrietta on and wearily headed up the sidewalk and up the steps to her house. Noticing Baskerville's window pet door was open a sliver, she reached over to push it all the way shut. It was stuck on something. On examining it closer, she found a small necklace wedged in the crack of the door, stopping it from entirely closing. Granny surmised that Baskerville had dragged the necklace home from the farm. George must have brought him home with him when he returned from the farm and dropped him off before going down to the police station. Lifting the necklace to eye height, Granny noted a *V* carved into the necklace.

All was quiet as Granny entered her house. It was 6:00 a.m., the shysters were gone for the day. Baskerville and Mrs. Bleaty must have headed out too, Granny decided. Rubbing her eyes, Granny knew she needed a long summer's nap. She couldn't remember the last time she'd been out all night. Part of her expected that her daughters would have been waiting for her when she got home after hearing of the events of the day. It was strange she hadn't heard from them. Usually, they would have been threatening to put her in the wrinkle farm by now. But...since Thor and

Penelope now lived in town, they were able to watch her every move. And Starshine and her fiancé, Lars, were looking for a place to live when they got married. They too would be living in Fuchsia. The thought crossed Granny's mind that maybe she should move. Her entire family living in Fuchsia might cramp her style.

Yawning, Granny headed to her bedroom to take a short nap. The house was so quiet it would be easy to sleep. Entering her bedroom, she saw Mrs. Bleaty and Baskerville both sleeping in front of her closet door. The door was open a few inches. She remembered she'd left it open yesterday morning in her hurry to help Angel. Usually, she kept it tightly closed so no one would snoop and find the hidden door in the closet.

"What are you two doing here? Isn't it your time to be at Silas house?" Granny asked the sleeping animals as she tried to nudge them aside so she could get into her closet to change into something more comfortable for her nap.

Baskerville lifted an eyelid but did not budge. Mrs. Bleaty moved her head closer to Baskerville, blocking Granny's foot.

"Okay, you two, move it! You never sleep here. I need to get into my closet."

Baskerville moved closer to Mrs. Bleaty. Mrs. Bleaty lifted her head and nudged Granny gently back.

"I need to get into my closet. Move it!" Granny instructed in a loud voice.

Both Baskerville and Mrs. Bleaty stood up together and backed Granny away from the closet.

"What is wrong with you two?"

Then Granny heard a movement in the closet. She stared hard at the small crack at the opening to her closet, backing up carefully to reach for her umbrella, only realizing that it was still in the basement where she'd left it the previous midnight. She looked around the room looking for a new weapon.

"You're protecting me. That's it!" she said to the animals.

Picking up her flip flop on the floor, she held it in her hand, ready to throw it at whatever was in the closet, when the door to the closet suddenly popped open and, quick as a flash, a creature bounded out of the closet and attacked Granny knocking her to the floor.

"What....ugh!" Granny managed to squeak out as slobbery kisses from a snout, peppered her face.

Pushing the medium-sized creature away, she looked into a piggy face. "Mr. Porky, what are you doing here? Baskerville, did you bring this creature home with you?" Granny asked as she got a hold on the pot belly pig that was greeting her. "Is this the pig from the farm?"

Taking her cell phone out of her pocket with one hand, while holding the exuberant pig at bay with the other, she belted into the phone, "Mavis!"

"Mavis and George, Detective Agency," came the response on the phone.

"Mavis, let me talk to George!"

"He's busy on a case, Granny."

"Mavis......I need to talk to George, now!"

"You stabem, we slabem," George answered, coming on the line.

"George, that slogan is for a funeral parlor not a detective agency and, besides, you and Mavis are not detectives!" Granny yelled. "Why did you bring this porker home with Baskerville? I have enough animals!"

"Porker? Animals? Baskerville?" George countered.

"George!"

"We didn't bring Baskerville home, Granny," said George on the phone, "Silas and I looked for him but he was long gone. We knew he'd find his way home. What porker are you talking about or did you say New Yorker?"

Granny slammed down the phone and picked it up again, paging through her contacts.

"Woodly!" Granny belted the name into the phone.

"Ah, ah," a yawn could be heard on the other end of the phone.

"Woodly, I need you to build me another building next to my house. When can you start?"

"Granny?" Woodly had been the contractor on her new garage and he recognized Granny's raspy, crotchety tone. "Do you know what time it is? It's 6:00 a.m."

"Time for young men like you to be up working. I'll meet you at Rack's at 5:00 p.m. to let you know what I want." Granny hung up the phone. Her eyes were feeling droopy. She'd deal with Baskerville and the porkster later. Having calmed down, the pig had followed Baskerville and Mrs. Bleaty into the kitchen while Granny had been on the phone. Now Granny returned to her bedroom, lay back on her bed and promptly fell asleep.

CHAPTER ELEVEN

A wet nose woke Granny up as she was dreaming that Gram Gramstead had her down in a headlock on her basement floor. Furball moved her nose from Granny's nose to Granny's head and began grooming her hair.

"Think my hair's messed up, do you? It must be late if you shysters are back from your investigations." Picking Furball off her face and head, Granny set her down next to her as she sat up. Picking up her cell phone that was by the bed, she noted that it was 4:30. She'd better hurry if she was going to meet Woodly Spackle at Racks.

She heard a sniff by her bedroom door and saw that the rest of the shysters were watching her. "Are you hungry?" The animals reacted to her question. Furball pawed her arm, Fish tickled her ankles with his paws, little white poodle jumped on Granny's lap and licked her face, and Tank stayed by the bedroom door, growling at some unknown entity down the hallway.

Standing up and gently dislodging the shysters from her body as she spoke, Granny said, "Have you seen a porky pig, Tank?"

Turning to Granny, Tank answered with an "aaarfgruff."

Shuffling past Tank, she indicated for them all to follow her.

Baskerville and Mrs. Bleaty were waiting for her in the kitchen watching Mr. Porkster try to open the refrigerator door. Granny bent down and got eye to eye with the pig. "Who are you and why were you locked in the basement? And…..who taught you how to get your own dinner by opening the refrigerator?" Mr. Porkster snorted at Granny and backed away from her hand.

Granny opened the refrigerator and got out the yogurt and the greens for the shysters, along with a tuna treat and a steak for Baskerville. Looking at Mr. Porkster, she murmured, "What do Pot Belly Pigs eat? I'll have to look that up. I think you like greens. I'll give you some for now."

Mr. Porkster snorted at Granny again and moved over to take the steak Granny was holding for Baskerville out of her hands.

"You want to eat a cow?" Granny asked perplexed.

Mr. Porkster grabbed the steak out of Granny's hand and ran to the trash bin, nudged it open and dumped it in. Baskerville let out a loud howl and followed Mr. Porkster to the trash bin. Mr. Porkster, blocked Baskerville from getting to the trash can to remove the steak.

Granny laughed. "Don't you want Baskerville to eat Mr. Cow? Okay, Baskerville, you're going to have to change your diet and eat like the shysters until I figure out new food for you."

Granny moved to the door and picked up her pocketbook. "I have to meet old Woodly. You're all going to have a new house. Have a good night on your rounds and don't bring me any more creatures. Got it?"

Closing the door after stepping out on her porch, Granny took a moment to gaze at the neighborhood. It was close to five in the afternoon and all seemed to be quiet. Her daughter Penelope and her husband Butch, who lived across the street and over a house, lived in George's old house. When Penelope and Butch had moved back to town, they'd bought Nail's Hardware Store, and they were probably still at work.

Mavis and George could be seen through their picture window re-enacting a cooking reality show. Mavis was always re-enacting something and now George was hooked too.

Glancing over at Silas's house on the other corner, catty-corner from her house, Granny could see no movement there. Cantankerous Silas, was probably out plotting against her again. He really knew how to get Granny's ire up. Some woman would be very unlucky to have him for a husband, and she was glad it wasn't her. Franklin was the guy for her.

Shaking herself out of her musings, she walked to her garage. She was glad to have her car back after a long winter. Granny sighed in happiness as she stepped into her garage. Until….there was no car! Where was her car? Did she forget it somewhere? She'd had it yesterday, hadn't she?"

Granny paced back and forth in the empty garage. No, it should be here! Her friends had taken her out through the underground streets the other day on her birthday. Her car should be here. Where was her car?

The tooting of a horn outside her garage got Granny's attention. She pushed the button to open the garage door. There in front of her garage was Amelia— in Granny's car!

Granny rushed over to the car and opened the driver's side door of the car. "You stole my car! What next? And to think I was going to help you find your son. You're a thief; Amelia! You stole my car just like you stole Robert Blackford from me!"

Amelia exited the car, pushing Granny back so Amelia had room to stand. Looking Granny straight in the eye, she said, "I did not steal your car, Granny. You left it in front of my house during the night."

"I did no such thing! I was at the police station all night. I can prove it. I have an alibi. It's called interrogation."

"You were at the police station? Why? This is your car, right?" asked Amelia.

"You stole my car!" cried Granny.

"No......you left it in front of my house with the keys in it," repeated Amelia. "You just forgot. I have heard from others that you're a little forgetful. Did I hear some talk of the wrinkle farm?"

Granny skewered Amelia with a glowering look as she scooted past her and sat down in the driver's seat. "If you want a ride, Amelia, get in. I'm going to be late."

Amelia hurried around the side of the car and hopped into the passenger side. "Where are we going?"

"You're going home since it's right across the street from Racks. I'm going to Racks!"

"Tell you what, Granny, I'll go with you and you can tell me why you might end up in an orange jumpsuit. Not really your color though," Amelia observed.

Granny raised her eyebrows before answering, "Fine, but I'm meeting Woodly Spackle to discuss some plans. We can't murder each other in public so it's probably a good place for you to tell me why you stole the love of my life. Don't talk until we get there, though. I have to concentrate on my driving."

Granny backed out of the driveway, came to a complete stop, then stomped on the foot pedal and peeled off down the street, screeching her tires.

Amelia had a look of terror in her eyes as they came to the first intersection. She was barely able to squeak out a scream and then, closing her eyes and gripping the arm rest, she suggested, "Perhaps I should drive, Granny."

"I said, don't talk—I'm concentrating." Granny rounded the curve, avoided the ice cream truck that was turning a corner a block down, tore around Fuchsia Town Square twice for fun, and took a short cut down a one-way street before turning into Rack's parking lot, and bringing the car to a complete halt.

"Now you can talk," Granny said.

CHAPTER TWELVE

"That's a beautiful tree over there in the parking lot. You should have parked under it; it would have kept the car cool," Amelia suggested, referring to the unique willow-like tree in the corner of the lot.

"Yep, gorgeous tree; it's the best place to park your car late in the afternoon," Granny advised with a smirk on her face, not telling her sister that the tree had unique properties. When darkness descended, the tree folded down on anything that was under it, and the car would be stuck until morning. "You should try it sometime; it's said to be good luck if you park there late in the afternoon. It's good karma. A canopy of warmth covers your vehicle and keeps you safe until morning."

Granny got out of the car and headed for the door of Rack's Restaurant, leaving Amelia to scramble out of the car to keep up with her sister.

Once inside, Granny headed for her favorite booth towards the back of the restaurant. It had a view of the street so Granny could keep her eagle eye trained on the happenings outside. Amelia scooted in next to Granny in the booth.

"You can't sit across from me?" asked Granny.

"You said you were meeting someone. I thought it would be easier. You don't want Franklin seeing you having supper with a strange man." Amelia gave Granny an innocent smile.

"Hi, Granny, I'd heard there were two of you. Does she eat like you?" asked the waitress.

"Amelia, this is Gretchen. Tell her what you like to eat and she'll remember it. And if you have to hide what you eat from your family, she'll help you there too." Granny was referring to the fact that when she was eating with her family, they always ordered her healthy food but she preferred fried chicken, fried onion rings, mashed potatoes and gravy, and a chocolate desert.

Amelia smiled at Gretchen, "I'd like fried chicken, mashed potatoes and gravy, fried onion rings and—do you have pork rinds?"

"No, no pork rinds for her! Amelia! A porky gave his life for those pork rinds!" Granny protested.

"I'll have the fried chicken, mashed potatoes and gravy—no, scratch that!" Granny said, scratching her head as she used those words. "I'll have the Caesar Salad and a bowl of vegetable soup."

Gretchen gave Granny a shocked look. "Are your children here somewhere?" She turned and looked to see if she spotted them.

"No, but a chicken gave his life too for our fried chicken," Granny reminded them both.

Confused, Gretchen nodded her head. "Okay...I'll get your order, ladies."

As Gretchen walked away, Woodly Spackle eased past her and slid into the booth across from Granny and Amelia.

With a frown, he stared at the two women. "Okay, which one of you is Granny?"

Granny and Amelia both grinned and said at the same time, "Me!" Laughing, they looked at one another.

Granny turned to Woodly and said, "We always did that to everyone when we were young, especially to our boyfriends. They never knew who they were taking out, and we never told them."

Realizing what she'd just said, the stern look came back on Granny's face. "Of course, that was a long time ago. Let's get down to business, Woodly. I want you to build me a unique small house next to mine towards the woods. I want it attached by a cute hallway to my kitchen. I will draw up the plans myself and get them to you. When can you start?"

"Next year?" suggested Woodly.

"Woodly Spackle, I happen to know that you dated the mayor's daughter. And she had the key to the mayor's office. You two would steal in there at night and who knows what went on. I'm sure I could convince the mayor that I know what went on. And I happen to know that you're still dating the mayor's daughter, even though she's Jack Puffleman's wife, and—you're still meeting at night in the mayor's office." Granny tapped her fingers on the table.

Woodly Spackle looked around to make sure that no one had heard what Granny had just said. When he was satisfied that his escapades with the mayor's daughter were still a secret, he turned to Granny, "I can start next week. You get me the plans."

Granny smiled. "Excellent."

"Well, uh I have to be going. See you next week." Woodly hurriedly left the booth and walked out of Rack's, but not before looking around to make sure the mayor or his wife were not in the vicinity.

Amelia turned and gave Granny a raised eyebrow look, while shaking her head in agreement, she said, "Now that was creative."

"It gets better. Can you keep a secret?" Granny asked in a hushed voice.

"You didn't know I was dating Robert Blackford, did you?"

Granny skewered her twin with a piercing look. "It wouldn't matter if I told the mayor that Woodly is seeing his daughter, because the mayor is seeing Woodly's wife, even though she's a decade younger than Horatio! It's a wonder they haven't run into each other at night in the mayor's office. It appears to be the spot to be hot."

Gretchen arrived at that moment with their meal, setting the plates down in front of the two women. Amelia slid out of the booth, moving across from Granny, so they could look each other in the eye as they ate and talked about their past.

Amelia took a bite out of her mashed potatoes before she thoughtfully looked at her sister. "Robert thought I was you."

"How could he think you were me? You were nothing like me. You looked like me and when we wanted to fool people, we acted like each other, but you were miss prim and proper and sweet. You were refined. That's why you were engaged to Ferdinand."

Amelia took a gulp of her coffee before answering. "Ferdinand was boring. I always admired your sassiness and your gift of adventure. You were momma's wild child and I was her milk toast. I always wanted to be you. Robert was so romantic and so handsome. He was daring and fun, and so I pretended to be you that week you were sick with pneumonia. I must admit it was fun and when he begged me to run off with him—I thought, why not?"

"And he couldn't tell the difference when he kissed you? That you weren't me?" Granny asked in disbelief.

"At first, he thought I was having second thoughts about running off with him and that was why I was a little standoffish. You know, according to him, you did run hot and cold depending on what you were scheming at the time. So he didn't think it too strange. And then…I knew. It turns out I can kiss as good as you!"

Granny stood up and slid out of the booth. She straightened up and stood as tall as she could for someone five feet tall. Pointing her finger at the window, she said, "See that house out the window, that's yours. When I sit here, I can keep an eye on it and, believe you me, I'll be keeping an eye on a traitor like you! I assume you can find your way home!"

Meeting Gretchen as she was making her way to the door, she instructed her, "Granny's back there; she'll pay the bill."

Once outside, Granny took a whiff of the summer air and decided to see if Franklin wanted to go for a ride. Putting the top down on her convertible, she got into the driver's seat, cranked up the radio and glanced at the window in the restaurant where she and Amelia had been sitting. Amelia was still there, head bowed as her hand wiped a tear from her eye.

Granny was about to pull out of the parking lot to go and visit Franklin, when she glanced back at Amelia still sitting in the booth. Amelia was no longer alone. Franklin was seated by her side, holding her in his arms as she cried on his shoulder.

Granny revved the engine and took off out of the parking lot, not caring that a police car was sitting on the corner of the block.

Soon Granny heard the siren. Looking back in her rear view mirror she saw the flashing lights behind her car. Sighing, she pulled over. To her surprise, instead of stopping to talk to her, the police car kept going, lights flashing, in the direction of Amelia's new chocolate factory. Granny decided to follow at a slow pace so they wouldn't know she was following them.

The police car pulled into the lot of the chocolate factory. She pulled up, across and down the street from the factory. Her car was partially hidden by the tree on the corner of the street.

Granny watched as other police cars came from all directions and congregated in the parking lot. Soon she saw Lars, Starshine's fiancé, come out of the factory and talk to the police. *What was Lars doing at the chocolate factory?*

Granny peered over the windshield of her convertible so she could get a better look at the scene. At the precise moment that she craned her neck up over the windshield, Franklin's car drove by with Amelia in the front seat. They were so busy talking that they failed to see Granny's car. Granny sat back down in the seat to wait to see how the excitement played out.

Soon Thor and the Tall Guy joined the scene, coming out from the back of the plant. *What was going on?*

Granny took her cell phone out of her pocket. "Heather!" she belted out her daughter-in-law's name. "Good evening, Heather. How are you?"

"Just fine, Mom Fiddlestadt, and you?"

"I was wondering if Thor was at home."

"No, no, he's not."

"Do you know where I can find him?"

"He's out on a case."

"Oh, that's interesting. Does it have anything to do with Robert Blackford and Amelia?"

Granny heard the other car door in her car slam shut, and felt the phone being taken out of her hand before Heather could answer her.

"Heather, Silas Crickett here. Never mind your mother-in-law. And don't bother Thor. I can get her out of the jam she's in this time. We'll talk later."

Silas hung up and handed the cell phone back to Granny.

"Trouble? I'm not in any trouble, you nosy old man," said Granny.

"You would be, if I wasn't always here to save you from yourself."

Granny sputtered, "Get out of here! You'll blow my cover. I need to find out what's going on at the factory."

"You could ask."

"Ask who? Thor?"

"No, me. Silas Crickett at your service," Silas said, chuckling at Granny's expression.

"And why would you know something?"

"I'm a former detective and I have a police scanner, and—I talked to Ephraim."

"Spill it!" Granny ordered.

"Not so fast. Why are you here?"

"I was having supper at Rack's. I'm going to expand my house so I had to meet Woodley Spackle, but that darn Amelia had my car so I had to give her a ride home. I was being nice like all of you told me I needed to be to my sister, and I invited her to join me for supper. But, she said something that upset me, so I left her at the restaurant. I was planning on going to see Franklin, but then the police led me here. Anything else? Now spill it."

"I suspect there's more to your story than there is to this story," Silas commented. "The alarm went off, but according to Lars it was a false alarm. The police needed to check to make sure."

"What is Lars doing there?"

"He's the general manager. He's Amelia's stepson."

"My daughter is engaged to Amelia's stepson and no one told me. You'd better get out of the car."

"Why would I do that?"

"Do you remember the snowmobile ride I gave you last winter in the snowstorm?"

Silas hesitated before he answered, "You mean the ride where you almost killed me and where you ran over a stiff?"

"That's it. If you don't want to repeat the ride then you'd better get out of my car."

Silas coughed, trying to hold it in but couldn't, and let out a belly-moving laugh. "There's no snow and there's no stiffs around, Granny. Good try."

Granny revved the engine and took off. "No, but there's ditches! Haven't you ever heard of ditch hopping?"

CHAPTER THIRTEEN

The sun was setting in the west as Granny drove out into the country, leaving the community of Fuchsia behind. Silas put his seatbelt on when he saw they were leaving the city and heard the words, "ditch hopping," not sure if Granny would make good on her threat, but Granny drove steady and was quiet during the drive. Silas decided he would not break the peaceful silence of the drive.

Twinkling stars dotted the sky as Granny turned into the driveway of her old home place. She parked the car in front of the house, the bright moon being the only light in the front yard that night. Both she and Silas sat quietly, neither breaking the stillness of the night. Only crickets made beautiful music in the background.

"He thought she was me. He thought he was running away with me," Granny said to the night air, forgetting that Silas was in the convertible with her.

Silas, knowing Granny was remembering, reached out with his hand to touch her hand that was still on the steering wheel, reminding her that she wasn't alone.

Feeling a hand on hers brought Granny out of her reverie. She turned to Silas. "How could he not tell the difference? My life would have been so different."

Silas still did not say anything.

"Did you see? Even today, she's trying to steal Franklin from me. He was with her tonight and, according to Pastor Henrietta, he was with Amelia when Pastor Henrietta was visiting her."

"I was there too, Hermiony. It was a visit. We were trying to find out information to help you. Why else would your paragon, Franklin, and I team up? It was all about you."

Granny sat back in her seat, looked up the stars, and then fixed her gaze on the dilapidated house. "Because she left, I had to marry Ferdinand. She was engaged to him at the time, you know. She was supposed to marry him."

"Well, maybe she did you a favor. Remember, it didn't work out too well for her. You have a family that you love and that loves you. It appears that her life with your Robert Blackford didn't last too long. You still had your mother and your father and your brothers. She lost it all because she wanted to be you."

"I stayed away from this farm because I wanted a new life—a life I chose, not one that was chosen for me. I didn't want any reminders. I didn't sell it because of the income from the rent and I wanted to have something I could hand down to my kids when I'm gone to help them out in their lives. Maybe, after everything that has happened in the last couple of days, I will find out I was wrong, and it will bring more heartache."

"I think you have to solve the case, Hermiony. What happened that the love of your life left your sister and ended up back here at your farm—dead, along with his sidekick?"

"I'm not sure I can solve it. Maybe I don't want to know what happened. Maybe it's time to give it all up, marry Franklin, and settle down into old age."

All of a sudden, Granny heard Silas slam his car door, saw her door open, and felt herself being pulled out of the car and gently pulled through the silo door.

"What, what are you doing Silas Crickett?" Granny sputtered as she tried to get out of his clutches. "Silas, are you going to murder me too? Did you do it?"

The moon was shining through the small window in the silo, giving off a little light so Granny could see the glint in Silas eyes. "Let me go! I'll find my pitchfork," Granny warned.

Silas laughed, grabbed Granny, and kissed her like she hadn't been kissed in years.

Granny took her hands and pushed against Silas's chest, moving herself away from him, but not before giving him a swat on his arm. "What are you doing? Have you gone mad? Wait till I tell Franklin or Thor or your son! You're a cantankerous, sniveling old man, preying on unsuspecting old women."

Silas laughed louder. "That's the Hermiony Vidalia Criony Fiddlestadt that I know. The Hermiony that doesn't let anyone get the best of her and certainly isn't ready to settle in to old age! Now, let's solve these crimes!"

Silas walked out of the silo, leaving Granny staring at his back. Before following Silas out of the silo, she gave a glance around to see if the old pitchfork was still there in case she needed it. Not finding it, she made a mental note to herself to never leave her birthday present pitchfork at home again.

Silas was sitting on the cracked front steps of the house waiting for Granny. "Has Amelia said why this Robert Blackford left her and why he took her son?"

"Sure, she told me yesterday while we were having our nails and hair done at the spa because we're such good friends," Granny answered sarcastically. "Has your son or Thor told you anything about why I have dead people on my farm?"

"They're having a hard time finding out why the two men were here. It appears that Robert Blackford was living in Canada under another name. That's probably why your sister's detectives didn't find him. You know, in those days they didn't have the technology they have now. They're working on finding out what connection Dickey Lee Hatchet had to Robert Blackford."

"Maybe Amelia knows and she isn't telling," Granny surmised.

"You need to find out. You need to make friends with your sister."

"I can't. She's after Franklin. She's trying to steal another fiancé from me. No, you're right, Silas!. I need to keep my enemies close. I need to save Franklin from her! Oh, no! Maybe she's pretending to be *me* when she's with Franklin!"

"There could never be two of you, Granny," said Silas. "She couldn't pull that off; she's too nice."

At the implication that she was the *not nice* twin, Granny stomped over to her car, got in and revved the engine, "If you want a ride back, you'd better get in or I'll leave you here for the coyotes to eat, Mr. Supercilious."

CHAPTER FOURTEEN

Franklin was waiting on the steps when Granny and Silas drove into her driveway. Silas immediately got out of the car, turning to Granny who made no move to exit the car.

"Gotta face the music sometime," Silas said, indicating with his head that Franklin did not look too pleased. "In case the record sticks, you know where I'll be." Nodding again to Franklin, Silas walked across the street to his house.

Granny pushed the garage door opener and gently eased her car into her garage. She took a breath, turned off the ignition, closed the garage door and looked at the stairs going to the turret of her garage. Getting out of the car, she climbed the steps to the turret. Looking down from the turret window she saw Franklin was still waiting on her front steps. She made a decision.

Opening one of the windows, she called out to Franklin, "Come on up! It's a beautiful night."

She saw Franklin move off his spot on the steps, heard the side door to the garage open, and listened to the heavy tread of his feet on the stairs.

"Hermiony, would you mind telling me where you were?" he said. "It's almost midnight. I was worried. You were out in your car; you weren't answering your phone—and with two dead bodies on your farm, I was afraid we might find yours next. And then....you come waltzing home with Silas Crickett!"

"I wasn't waltzing; I was ditch hopping."

"Ditch hopping!" Franklin's exclamation was as loud as loud could be without him actually screaming at his fiancé.

"Do you think I'm too old for ditch hopping Franklin?" Granny challenged with a sweet tone.

"Yes, yes, I do. You could have broken your neck and I'm going to break Crickett's neck for egging you on. It was probably his idea."

"Relax, the idea was there, but all I did was go for a drive. I saw you with Amelia. Did you know it was Amelia and not me?" she asked.

"What kind of a question is that? Of course, I knew it was Amelia. Why would I think she was you? She was upset for some reason and then she got a call that the alarm was going off at her chocolate factory. I offered her a ride. And what's this about you misplacing your car again? Amelia said you left your car at her place in the middle of the night."

"Franklin, you see those stars up there?" Granny pointed to the stars. "You see that cemetery back there?" Granny pointed to the cemetery.

Franklin looked toward where Granny was pointing. "Ah, yes."

"We'd better enjoy the stars before our bodies are six feet under and we're one of those stars." Granny moved closer to Franklin, stood up on her tippy toes, since he was such a large man, wound her arms around his neck and gave him a big smooch.

Franklin, taken aback by Granny's uncharacteristic action, was caught off balance and fell back against the window screen. As he hit the screen, it fell out of the window and the top of his large body toppled out the opening, with his feet catching the sides of the window frame, leaving Franklin dangling from the turret upside down.

"Franklin! Franklin! You're falling for me!" Granny said tartly, grabbing at his feet to keep him from going any farther out the window. "I had no idea I had that kind of effect on you!"

Franklin grabbed her arms and she pulled him back into the turret.

"What has gotten into you, Hermiony? First you run off with Silas, and then you overwhelm me with passion so much that it knocks me off balance and I almost end up splattered on the ground."

Granny laughed. "I wanted to knock you off your feet and I guess I did."

"More like you were trying to distract me so you didn't have to answer my questions. Oh, well, never mind. I actually came by with some news about Robert Blackford."

Granny gave a sigh and turned to the steps. "All right, Franklin; let's go sit on the porch like two old people."

"Woo hoo!" Mavis yelled from across the street as they came out of the garage. "Everyone okay over there? We saw Franklin hanging from the turret window. That was a great stunt! You'll have to show us how you did that sometime. Did you have special shoes?"

Penelope happened to be taking out the trash at the same time that Mavis was hollering. "Mom, is that you? What are you doing up so late?" Then, seeing Franklin through the light that was shining down on the neighborhood from the moon, she nodded her head in understanding. "Mavis, it's late; maybe we should leave mom and Franklin alone."

"Hey, Penelope!" George piped up. "Where's Butch? Come on out and we'll light up the fire pit."

"George!" Mavis admonished, "Didn't you hear Penelope? Franklin and Granny want to be alone."

"I've got the portable fire pit," Silas interjected, walking across the street hauling a metal fire pit. "George, I could use some help."

"Got ya!" George hurried to help Silas. "Anyone got any marshmallows?"

"What did I just say, Silas?" Penelope asked. "Don't you know the meaning of the word *alone*?"

"They were just alone and she tried to throw him off the turret. Besides, he's got a wandering eye for Amelia. You don't want your mom to be suckered, do you, Penelope?" Silas challenged.

"Fine, come on, Butch! We'll chaperone these old people," Penelope said as Butch stuck his head out the door to see what all the yelling was about.

Mavis ducked back into her house for a second.

Franklin looked at Granny. "It's time for you to move to my house, Hermiony. It's a lot quieter at my Victorian—not so many nosy neighbors."

"I can't move to your house, Franklin, I'm building on to mine. Starts next week," Granny smugly announced.

"We're not living here after we get married. Do you understand, Hermiony?"

"You're not married yet, so I venture this ornery old woman can build whatever she wants!" Silas put his two cents worth in.

Franklin was about to reply when Mavis joined the group. "Didn't want to have a party without Ditty Belle and Delight so I called them. They'll be right over. Delight said she's bringing a new Pink Percolator cold drink for us to try. Silas, she said she named it after you." Mavis plunked down her lawn chair.

"She never names anything after me!" George complained.

A bleat and some barks could be heard in the distance. "It sounds like the shysters and the cohorts are on their way," said Granny. "They must have realized you weren't home yet, Franklin, and decided to come back here." Granny stood and looked toward the back of the house as the animals appeared from the direction of the Fuchsia Cemetery.

Delight and Ditty Belle arrived at the same time as Fish, Little White Poodle, Furball and Tank. Then Baskerville and Mrs. Bleaty joined the party. Radish was riding on Mrs. Bleaty's head.

Granny scowled. "You let that bird out now that it's summer? He's going to end up in the birdskow, Silas. After all, his language isn't always the best."

At the mention of his name, Radish jumped off of Mrs. Bleaty and landed on Delight's shoulder. Delight reached into her box and took out a red-beaded confection and gave it to the bird. "It's my new treat for birds, named after you, Radish. It's called Radish Razzle Dazzle! I thought it would be fun to branch out with my goodies."

Radish, plucked the morsel from Delight's hand and squawked, "Awk, it's a ravish."

Delight giggled. "Silas taught him that. Silas always tells me I'm ravishing, especially, when I give him an extra cup of Boneyard Specialty Coffee."

Granny's scowl became more pronounced as she looked at Silas, but before she could say anything, Little White Poodle dropped a tiny ring at her feet. Granny stooped down and picked it up to examine it. "What did you bring me now? Where did you steal this, Little White Poodle?"

Granny turned the ring over in her hand and held it close to the fire in the fire pit for light so she could examine it more closely. "There are initials on this ring. I think they are *V. B.*"

The women gathered around Granny to look at the ring.

"Who's *V. B.?*" Ditty Belle wondered.

"Victor Borge? He was a wonderful old movie star," Mavis added.

Penelope shook her head and laughed. "Maybe the shysters visited Antiquities Antique Shop today. You know, she's always letting them in and giving them treats. Since it's right across the street from the hardware store, I've watched her lure them in."

The four men were sitting around the fire pit listening to the musings of the women.

"More likely they've been back scrounging around at the farm. You know how they are once they find someplace new. They're relentless in exploring," Franklin reminded everyone.

Granny settled down on the front step. "Well, I guess that's a mystery for another time."

The fire's glow and Delight's new Silas Sizzler lulled everyone into an easy conversation about the celebration that would take place at the end of the summer in Fuchsia.

"What's the date for the Polar Bear Festival this year?" George asked.

Ditty Belle got out her cell phone and looked at her calendar. "It's at the end of August. I'm on the Polar Bear committee and we decided we'd have it the week before school started."

"Polar Bear Festival?" Silas's puzzled voice asked. "I know I'm new to this town, but I have to ask why would you have a Polar Bear Festival in the summer?"

Ditty Belle, confused by the question, answered, "Because we have the Pink Flamingo Festival at Christmas."

"Wouldn't it make more sense to celebrate flamingos in the summer and polar bears in the winter?" Silas suggested.

"Silas," Delight explained, not understanding why Silas was confused. "We can't celebrate polar bears in the winter. Everything's white and no one would see them. You can see flamingos in the winter. And in the summer, everything is colored, so you can see the white of the polar bears in the summer. It makes perfect sense."

"We're new too," Butch agreed and winked at Silas. "When you're in Fuchsia, act like the Fuchsians. Polar Bear Festival it is! Bring it on!"

They all raised their glasses to toast.

"Oh, my goodness; it's almost 2:00 a.m. This is the second night this week we've been out so late," Ditty Belle acknowledged.

Penelope raised her eyebrows at Ditty Belle's statement and looked pointedly at her mother. "Yes, you old people won't wake up for a month being out so late. Maybe it'll keep you out of trouble."

"Well, at least this time we didn't end up in the hoosegow," Granny reminded them.

"Speaking of the hoosegow, I do have some news to tell all of you about the case." Franklin moved in closer so all could hear.

"I think you all know that the reason Amelia couldn't find Robert Blackford was that he moved to Canada and used an alias. He was living off the grid. That was why she couldn't find him. Thor and the Tall Guy found out tonight that Dickey Lee Hatchet is the brother of Robert Blackford. Dickey Lee Hatchet has been in prison and was just released recently. Why the two brothers were holed up at Hermiony's is anyone's guess," Franklin concluded.

"Why didn't you just ask Amelia since you see her so often, Franklin," Granny taunted.

"She doesn't know, Hermiony," replied Franklin. "And you could be a little easier on her. She doesn't have a mean, deceiving, calculating bone in her body. She's very sweet."

"She pretended to be me and she stole my fiancé, Franklin!. Do you know what a chameleon is? They can change colors and look in two different directions at the same time—kind of like Silas."

A loud belly laugh came from Silas. "I'll be your chameleon, Granny; you can be my kaleidoscope. But I can guarantee you that the only direction I would look would be yours."

"Ooooh!" Ditty Bell, Mavis, and Delight all gushed at the same time. Butch winked at Penelope.

Granny was going to comment on Silas's words when Silas turned around and walked away, calling Radish to follow him.

"Aawk! Time for bed! Time for bed!" screeched Radish, flying after Silas.

The others, seeing the look on Franklin's face, decided to leave, muttering their goodnights as they went back to their respective houses. Delight and Ditty Belle got into their car, honked the horn and drove away, leaving Franklin and Granny standing on the front lawn alone.

"Well, that was fun, "Granny remarked.

"It would have been more fun if Silas Crickett would have stayed home. You have to stay away from him, Hermiony. Luckily, when we're married you'll live across town."

"Good night, Franklin," Granny said sweetly, giving him a peck on the cheek as she turned to walk up the steps to her porch.

"One more thing, Hermiony. The initials *V. B.* stand for Vitele Blackford. He's Amelia's son—the son Robert took from her when he left. I'm going to help her find him."

"You do that, Franklin. I'll help too. But you'd better be careful. Remember, Amelia can turn into me in a minute. Mama always called me the wild child and Amelia milk toast, but I really think Amelia's toast is more French—like in *oo la la*. You might just end up with your toast burnt."

CHAPTER FIFTEEN

Sunday morning Granny woke up refreshed and ready to go to services at We Save You Christian Church. She hadn't heard Pastor Henrietta's sermons yet. However, she had it on good authority (Ditty Belle) that this was Pastor Henrietta's week to preach. At We Save You a different denomination preached each week. The church was always full because each Sunday's service was a surprise. Congregation members never knew which denomination they were attending on any given Sunday. It could be a Catholic Service, a Lutheran Service, a Methodist Service or more. We Save You was the only church in Fuchsia. There was no need for any more churches since We Save You catered to everyone.

After their Friday night chit chat on the front lawn, everyone was tired, so Saturday had been a laid back day. Granny left her cell phone in the house, took her lawn chair and plopped herself in the middle of the trees and lawn in her back yard to read. She had quite a forest now since Gram Gramstead and her son had tried to make her into a thief by stealing the forest out of Ella's Enchanted Forest and planting it in her back yard while Granny was out hooking crooks.

Granny was always a little tearful when she first would sit in her yard, because the grass that Sally Katilda had lovingly given her before she'd died still came up green every year on the mound where it had been planted. It held a special place in Granny's heart. She'd placed a knitting needle as decoration on the mound of grass to remember that she had caught Sally's murderer, skewering the scoundrel who was responsible for Sally's death.

Granny plopped her hat on her head and straightened her colorful dress. Now that she was no longer working undercover, she decided a red dress in a flowing gypsy style would be perfect to wear to church. After reading *A Nate To Remember* by Barbara Jean Coast and noting the fashions in the book, she thought she might transport herself back to the 50's or the 60's. After all, she never got to wear any fashionable outfits when she was younger because country girls didn't dress up.

Granny surveyed herself in the mirror. She put on her sparkly high-top tennis shoes. They went well with the flowing dress.

As she was leaving home, Granny noticed that the shysters and the cohorts weren't around. Granny remembered that Mr. Pigster hadn't been with them last night. She hoped he was fine. Maybe she should check to see if he was back out on the farm. If he was, she'd bring the pot belly pig back home, since Robert had apparently been taking care of him. Robert was like that, Granny remembered, kind and always taking care of strays.

Penelope and Butch were getting into their car to head to church as Granny came out of her house.

"Mom, why don't you ride with us and we can chat?" Penelope gestured for her come over.

Granny made her way across the street. "Don't trust me to go to church, Penelope?"

Butch answered for Penelope, "No, we're saving the streets and potholes from your lead foot."

Granny settled into the back seat and wrinkled her nose at her son-in-law, turning her attention to Penelope. "What do you hear from my adorable grandchildren?"

"Penny and Bernard are fine. They'll be home for your wedding, whenever you and Franklin set the date. They were excited to hear it was finally on again."

"As long as Amelia doesn't get her hooks into him. Maybe I should lend her my umbrella so she can hook someone else."

Penelope admonished her mother, "Can't you let bygones be bygones, Mom? She's your sister. What would you say if Starshine and I didn't get along?"

Before Granny could answer, Butch put in his two cents worth, "I'd be more worried about Delight than Amelia, Granny. I think she likes Franklin. Don't you see her gushing every time she's around him? A man knows these things."

Penelope swatted Butches arm. "Don't give her any more ideas."

The parking lot was full when they reached the church. Butch let the women out in front while he went to park the car.

"Granny, Granny, you're here!" Angel skipped up to Granny, with Penelope, Thor and Heather following.

"I am, my sweet Angel!" said Granny to her granddaughter, "Are you going to sit by me?"

"I promised Aunt Amelia I'd sit by her so she wouldn't be alone. Will you sit by us?" Angel asked.

Heather broke into the conversation, "Yes, Granny, why don't you sit by us? Amelia brought Lars. Lars is also here with Starshine."

"Did Starshine know? Is this a plot? I wonder. Did she know all along that Lars was Amelia's stepson?" Granny asked with a scowl on her face.

"We don't know," said Heather. Thor looked at his pregnant wife and took her arm gently. "We have to sit, Mom," said Thor, "This new grandchild of yours will be here soon and Heather won't admit that she's uncomfortable standing too long."

Angel took Granny's hand. "Come on, Granny, let's go find Amelia."

Walking into the church with Angel, hand in hand, Granny was surprised to see Tricky Travis Trawler sitting in one of the pews. Tricky always liked to pilfer from the collection plate, and Granny always made sure she had her umbrella along to hook him before his hand did any pilfering. She should have brought her umbrella or her pitchfork, but both were back in her car in the garage at her house.

"Um, Angel, you go ahead and find Aunt Amelia. I have to sit next to Travis." Granny watched until Angel found Amelia, and then she moved to the pew where Tricky Travis Trawler was sitting and sat down next to him.

"Tricky, when did you get out of jail? I thought the milk caper at Pickles might have kept you away in the hoosegow for a while."

"Um, well, I didn't go to jail, I went to kleptomaniac rehab."

"What?" Granny asked in disbelief. "I've never heard of such a thing."

"Well, it exists and I'm cured. You don't have to sit next to me."

At that moment, Amelia, Angel, Lars and Starshine wove into the other side of the pew and sat down on the other side of Travis. Travis looked at Amelia and then looked at Granny. He reached over and pinched Granny's arm.

"I'm having delusions. I'm seeing two of you! It must be the drugs." Travis became agitated.

"Drugs," Granny agreed.

"Yes, you know the marijuana-type thing. They told me it was incense and it would relax me. It must really have lasting effects." He pinched Granny again.

"Ouch!" Granny jumped at getting pinched again. "Pinch her and see if she's real!" she said, motioning toward Amelia.

Travis reached over and pinched Amelia who pretended not to have heard the conversation.

Amelia didn't flinch or utter a word.

Travis turned back to Granny, "She didn't say anything. She must not be there."

Amelia leaned over and whispered to Travis, "I'm here, but no one else can see me and so I feel no pain. I'm your guardian angel sent to see that you have changed your ways."

Granny coughed to cover the laughter that was bubbling up in her throat. She leaned over to Travis, "Shh! Pastor Henrietta is starting the service. Do I need to watch you with the collection plate?"

Tricky Travis Trawler looked at Granny and then he turned and looked at Amelia and shook his head, "I promise; I've repented. I will steal no more." Travis then raised his hands to the air and bowed his head as if in prayer.

Granny glanced at Amelia at the same time that Amelia glanced at Granny. Granny glanced quickly away, but held Amelia's glance long enough to see her wink. Granny winked back before picking up her hymnal.

After the service, Granny shook Pastor Henrietta's hand before leaving the church. "Outstanding sermon, Pastor Henrietta, I especially liked the part where you reminded us that we are our brother's keeper. I should call my brothers and tell them we weren't called to be our sisters' keepers."

"Ah, Granny, that isn't exactly what it meant." Pastor Henrietta was going to say more but decided to save it for another time.

"Granny, will you take me out to your farm?" Angel begged.

"I'm not sure that's such a good idea, Angel, I don't think your mom or Thor would approve."

Thor, having overheard the question as he and Heather moved to join the two answered, "I think it's fine. You should take Franklin along, just in case, but the crime scene is clear."

Angel frowned. "The seen is clear? What did you seen, Thor?"

Heather laughed. "That's not quite what he meant, but if Granny wants to take you, that's fine, but only if Dad goes along."

"Where am I going?" Franklin asked, joining the group.

"Grandpa, will you and Granny take me out to see her farm?"

Franklin caught Granny's eye and saw her nod in agreement. "I guess we can do that. We can go right now and when we get back, we can stop at the Pink Percolator for ice cream."

"I'm going for ice cream! I'm going for ice cream!" Angel sang in a sing-song voice while skipping to her grandfather's car.

Franklin took Granny's arm and turned to Thor, "I'll see they both get home safely."

"And I'll see that Franklin stays out of trouble," Granny added. Tricky Travis Trawler happened to be walking by. "Just like Tricky Travis. He's never going to be in trouble again."

Travis looked at Granny and then past Granny to where Amelia was standing underneath an apple tree, "An apple doesn't fall far from the tree," Travis muttered, looked at Granny and looked at Amelia. "Do you see you over there?" he asked.

Granny's eyes met Amelia's across the parking lot. "I think that incense got to you, Travis, or maybe you're seeing your guardian angel come down to take you home. There's only one of me. Come on, Franklin, Angel's waiting." She tugged Franklin's arm so he'd walk with her.

Frowning, Franklin asked, "What was all that about?"

"Just Tricky Travis going straight," Granny said with a smile, "nothing for you to worry your handsome head about."

CHAPTER SIXTEEN

"Granny, did you have horses and pigs and dogs and cats and sheep and chickens?" Angel asked, standing outside the car and surveying the yard of the abandoned farm.

"A few, and some cows too," Granny answered, walking toward the house, stopping underneath the tree that she and her brothers used to climb when they wanted to sneak out of the house.

"Is this the tree you used to climb, Granny?"

"I wouldn't ask her that, Angel. She might think she can still climb it," Franklin challenged.

"Can you, Granny? Can you? Can I climb it?"

"Maybe another time, Angel; we've still got our church clothes on." Granny pointed to one of the windows on the second floor of the house by the tree. "That used to be my room. It was right over the porch. That's why we could get to the tree. I used to climb out on the porch at night and wish on the stars."

"Did Aunt Amelia wish too?" Angel asked.

In a faraway voice Granny answered, "Yes, Angel, Aunt Amelia wished too."

"What did you wish for?"

Franklin took Angel's hand. "Don't you know you aren't supposed to tell your wishes, Angel, or they won't come true. Let's go look in the silo."

"Hmm, the door's open. The police must not have closed it the other night," Granny guessed.

Franklin moved into the silo with Angel still holding his hand. Turning to Granny and giving her a warning look, he said, "Angel, I think you and Granny should get in the car. It's time to go get some ice cream."

"But I want to play in the haystack!" Angel announced as she broke away from Franklin's grip and ran toward the hay.

Franklin made a quick grab and caught Angel up in his arms at the same time that Granny made an observation. "Hay? The last time I was here, they took all the hay away."

All of a sudden at the noise, the hay began to ripple.

"Get Angel out of here, Franklin! I'll take care of this," Granny announced, picking up the pitchfork that was sitting by the door.

Before either of them could move, the mound of hay parted and Mr. Pigster shook the hay off his body, waddled up to Granny, and snuffled her dress.

Granny laughed and put the pitchfork down. "What are you doing back here? I was going to look for you."

"Granny, be careful, he'll snort you!" Angel warned while cuddling closer to her grandfather.

"Come here, Angel," said Granny. "This is a pot belly pig; we're going to take him home with us."

"We are?" Franklin asked, lowering Angel to the floor.

"Yes, we are," replied Granny. "Baskerville has taken a shine to Mr. Pigster, and since he's here, he must not have an owner. I think he may have belonged to Robert Blackford or that Dickey Lee Hatchet. And now that they're . . . um . . . visiting another land—" improvised Granny, not wanting to announce their demise in front of Angel.

"We're going to have to build them their own house on my property, Hermiony, if you keep acquiring more cohorts," Franklin warned.

"Did you not hear that *I'm* building a home for them as an addition onto my house, Franklin? Where did this hay come from anyway? Do you suppose the police returned it? And the pitchfork was back. I looked for it the other night and it wasn't here."

"It's a good thing I brought my Escalade. It's big enough so your Mr. Pigster will fit inside. He better not use my vehicle for a litter box," Franklin answered, ignoring Granny's questions.

"He can sit next to me by my car seat. See he likes me!" Angel suggested as Mr. Pigster gave her a kiss on her nose with his snout.

Franklin was about to get into his car when he spied something red in the bushes. "That couldn't have been there the other night. The police scoured this property." Walking over to the bush, he plucked out a red wig and brought it back to the car.

Holding the wig with one hand, he shook it in front of Granny's face. "Did any of you women by any chance lose your wig when you were partying out here the other night?"

Granny's face turned white. She grabbed the wig out of Franklin's hand. "Gram Gramstead! She's behind this. This is her wig, remember! She must be back and out to get me. She's up to her old tricks. She's probably the one who stole my car and left it at Amelia's. Maybe she and Amelia are in cahoots." Lowering her voice so Angel wouldn't hear, she whispered, "Maybe they're a team and murdered Robert and his brother."

Franklin shook his head. "Can't be, Hermiony. She's in prison. All locked up. This wig probably blew in from the neighbors. And your sister Amelia does not have a conniving bone in her body. You need to get over your paranoia."

CHAPTER SEVENTEEN

The Pink Percolator was filled with families treating their kids to ice cream on the warm Sunday afternoon. Not only did Delight serve coffee and confections, in the summer time, she opened an ice cream counter and served the most unique ice cream brands and flavors she could find.

Franklin led Angel and Granny to the patio where there were still some seats available because people were taking advantage of the air-conditioning inside, but Angel always liked to sit on the donut-shaped patio and watch the fountain that made the center of the donut. Today it was running pink cream water, reminding people of an ice cream soda.

"Hi, Granny! Franklin and little Angel! Specialty coffee for you, Granny? Rickety tea for you, Franklin? And a marshmallow, chocolate and raspberry delight malt for you, Angel?" Ella, Delight's daughter, asked when she came to take their order.

Granny skewered up her nose in thought, "No, I think I'll have a triple delight chocolate, strawberry, banana, raspberry, butterscotch whirlawhip."

"Granny, my dad wouldn't approve," Angel advised. "He said you have to eat healthy so we can keep you alive."

"Angel, did you hear the strawberry, banana, raspberry part of it? That's all very healthy." Granny nodded her head in agreement with her statement.

Franklin raised his eyebrows. "When did Delight get a WhirlaWhip machine? I haven't had one of those since Hanson Drug Store had its Soda Bar in the '60's back in my old home town. I haven't seen one since. I'll have a chocolate whirlawhip!"

"I didn't even know what it was until Mom got one," Ella explained. "But it's all the rage now here in Fuchsia. That Hanson Drug Store had something back then. Their WhirlaWhip machine must have been gold."

"You haven't seen someone who looks like Gram Gramstead or Mrs. Shrill around here lately have you, Ella?"

At the words *Gram Gramstead* and *Mrs. Shrill*, Ella dropped her order pad and pencil on the floor. "Why would she be here? She's in jail, right?" remembering how she had been kidnapped and nearly killed at the hands of Gram Gramstead.

Franklin shook his head picked up her pad and pencil. "Calm down, Ella. Granny is just paranoid; that's all. Put it out of your mind."

Ella walked away, muttering to herself. "Breathe, breathe, breathe; no more crooks."

Granny waved to Starshine and Lars, who'd just come out onto the patio. "Yoo hoo! Come and join us!" she cried.

Starshine came over to the table, kissed her mom on the cheek, hugged Angel, nodded to Franklin and turned to say something to Lars when she noticed that he wasn't behind her. Frowning, she said, "I wonder where he went?"

"Looks like he's over there, talking to Ella."

"Yes; you know he helped out here for a while until the factory was built."

"Starshine, you didn't tell me that Lars was my step-nephew, and your step-cousin," Granny scolded.

"What? My step-cousin?" Starshine asked, confused.

"You didn't know? He lied to you?"

Glancing over to where Lars was talking to Ella, Starshine shook her head. "She's probably imagining things again. Do you know that I heard from Penelope that she forgot her car in front of Aunt Amelia's the other night?"

Franklin squirmed in his seat and cleared his throat before saying, "Starshine, it…..appears…..that your fiancé is Amelia's stepson." Leaning back in his chair he waited for Starshine's reaction.

Starshine was silent for a minute. She looked over at Lars. Then she looked at Granny and said in her usual calm, hippie-child fashion, "The stars have spoken. Lars and I have found each other and, you, mom, have found a nephew. I'm sure that he was just waiting until the universe felt it was right to tell me."

Granny tipped her head and gave Starshine a skeptical look. "Well, what do you suppose the universe is saying that is causing your fiancé or, if you will, my step-nephew, to be so engrossed in conversation with Ella? Perhaps there are more things he's not telling you."

Granny stood up and marched over to where Lars was talking to Ella. "Ella, is our order going to be ready soon or do I have to whirlawhip it into shape myself? Lars, outside! We need to have a few words."

Lars, looking confused, nodded his head at Ella and followed Granny to the front of the Pink Percolator and out the door.

Starshine, seeing what was happening, got up to follow Granny. Franklin stopped her. "Sit down. He's going to have to learn how to handle his aunt or his mother-in-law—or should they turn out to be one and the same—both."

Angel, listening to the entire conversation, finally piped up with her thoughts, "Lars is Dad's step-step cousin because Dad is my step-dad, and he will be my step-uncle because he's marrying my Aunt Starshine and she's my step-aunt. That's a lot of steps!" Smiling, she turned to her grandfather. "But you're my real grandfather and Granny will be my step-grandmother too. I wonder if she likes steps?"

Franklin and Starshine laughed. "Yes, it is," said Franklin, "but we'll figure it all out, Angel! Look! Here's your ice cream and here comes Granny and Lars."

Granny sat back down while Lars pulled up a chair.

"Lars, did you forget to tell me something?" Starshine asked gently.

Lifting a spoonful of ice cream and strawberries to her mouth, Granny paused the spoon halfway to her mouth "It's all straightened out, Starshine. You can marry him. We understand one another."

Looking confused, Franklin spoke up, "What does that mean?"

"It means you're all on a need to know basis and none of you need to know!" said Granny.

Lars looked Starshine in the eyes after looking to Granny and seeing her nod, he said, "Yes, Starshine, you don't need to know what was said outside, but your mother and I have come to an understanding. I am Amelia's stepson and it's a long story. When the time is right, I'll tell you the story. Can you trust me?"

Starshine sat perfectly still, moving only her eyes back and forth from Lars to Granny, trying to figure out what was going on.

Franklin, on the other hand, was not so accepting, "Hermiony, what are you up to now? What did you say to Lars? What do we only need to know on a need to know basis?"

Ignoring Franklin, Granny stood up. "Angel, we have to get you home. Good luck on your house hunt, Starshine!" Turning to Franklin, she indicated that it was time to leave. "That's why they're in town; they're house hunting. Maybe you should sell them your Victorian, Franklin, so you can move into my house when we get married!"

Granny was out the door with Angel before Franklin could mutter a retort. He'd bought that Victorian house for him and Granny. And by George! They were going to live in it!

CHAPTER EIGHTEEN

Franklin and Granny dropped Angel off at her home, and stopped to visit for a few minutes with Heather and Thor. It was late afternoon. Heather invited Granny and Franklin to stay for supper, but they declined, noting the tired lines around Heather's eyes from the discomforts of her pregnancy. Both Granny and Franklin were excited about welcoming a new grandchild into the world.

Granny didn't have a chance to ask Thor more about the murders and Robert Blackford because she didn't want to upset Angel. However, it appeared Angel had other ideas.

"Daddy, Grandpa found a red wig out at Grandma's farm and Grandma freaked out. Grandpa told her she was par-a-par-a—paranoid. What does that mean?"

Thor looked at his soon-to-be father-in-law and shook his head. "It means, my sweet girl, that sometimes Granny sees something that isn't there."

Angel's eyes widened. She moved next to Granny on the couch. "Did you see a ghost on your farm?"

Granny gave Thor a whose-got-the-imagination-now look. "You could say that, Angel."

"Can we go ghost hunting the next time we go to your farm, Granny?" Angel popped up off the couch, jumping up and down in excitement.

"I think it's time for us to go home," Franklin announced, gently grabbing Granny's arm and hustling her out of the house. "Let us know if Heather goes into labor, Thor," he said at the door.

Back in the car, Franklin was silent.

"Well, since I'm so *paranoid*, you'd better take me home. Angel's ghosts might get you," Granny said sarcastically.

Franklin drove the couple of blocks to Granny's house while remarking on the new color the Fuchsia Street Department had painted on all the city street curbs. "I wasn't sure painting the curbs lining the streets a bright fuchsia was going to work, but I guess since they lined the curb where it meets the street with white, it really pops. That's scary; I'm getting used to the way this community does things. It has almost knocked the New Yorker out of me," he said.

"Well, I see someone who's going to get the Alaska knocked out of him. What is Silas Crickett doing on my lawn? It looks like he's putting stakes in the ground. Is he some sort of vampire?"

Granny quickly exited the car, almost before it had come to a complete stop, not allowing Franklin time to answer her comment.

"Silas Crickett, what are you doing to my yard?"

"I'm staking my claim, Granny."

Franklin, hearing Silas's words as he caught up to Granny, reached over and took the stake from Silas hands. "You lost your stake a long time ago, Crickett. This isn't Alaska, and Granny isn't your property!"

With a shrewd glint in his eye, Silas explained, "I was staking out Granny's new addition. Woodly Spackle told me about Granny's plans for her addition and showed me the plans Granny had drawn. I had an idea that I thought might work better for the shysters and the cohorts and Mr. Pigster."

Franklin looked at Granny. "We need to discuss this. Is it really worth adding on when you'll be moving soon?"

"Do you have a wedding date set?" Silas smirked.

"Instead of you two arguing about my life, maybe you'd better help the Fuchsia Police Department and your son and son-in-law solve these murders so I can sleep at night. Since you both used to be such hot shot detectives, you should be able to read the clues. I'm going to snooze. Good night!"

Granny didn't glance back as she climbed the porch steps and entered her house. All was quiet with the shysters and the cohorts, home from their day's snooping, covering the carpet with their bodies, their gentle snoring making background music in the room.

Granny decided that although it was early, she needed her sleep. She'd lost a lot of sleep the last couple of days, and she missed her dreams. Maybe she'd dream about getting another key to the city.

Once in her bedroom, she pulled out her latest purchase from Red Hot Momma's Boutique. It was a red silk chemise gown with see-through webbing on the side and trimmed in pink sequins. Embroidered on the front of the silky gown were the words *Hot Diva*.

Opening the secret door of her closet, she pulled out her red, silk flip-flops trimmed in fur. Her kids didn't want her to flip or flop so they forbid her from wearing flip-flops. Because of their disapproval, Granny reserved a special place in her secret closet to stash all her different versions of flip-flops. Digging toward the back of the secret closet, she came out with a box of chocolates and a bottle of wine. She usually kept her wine in the false bottom of the footstool, but the special wine that she saved for bedtime was stashed in the back of her closet. Looking at the bottle of Sizzle from the Fuchsia winery, she sighed. Chocolates and wine and a good book. What more could a woman ask for?

Crawling into bed, she pulled out the book she'd been reading, *The History of Fuchsia Minnesota*. She was so young when Robert Blackford lived in Fuchsia.

A teenager didn't care about a boy's parents or his background. All she'd seen were his beautiful blue eyes and gorgeous copper-colored hair. All he had to do was look at Hermiony and her heart melted. She wondered what the police had found out about his background and that of this Dickey Lee Hatchet. She didn't remember that name as one from her past. Maybe this history book would shed light on some of his ancestors and other Fuchsotans.

After a few minutes of reading, Granny's eyes began to close. It didn't seem to matter that it was only 8:00 p.m. and still daylight out. Putting her book down, she fell into a dream-filled sleep.

In her dream, there was horrible pounding. The pounding got louder. Mayor Horatio Helecourt pounded his gavel on the podium. Chaos erupted as he announced that Silas Crickett would be the new Mayor of Fuchsia. Silas was closing the underground streets so he could use them for his own private corporation, The Alaskan Radish Group.

Granny's dream ended as the pounding doubled and finally woke her up. Opening her eyes, she realized someone was again pounding on the door to the underground streets. Swinging her feet to the ground and holding the bedpost so she didn't sway when she first stood up, she grabbed her cell phone by the bed and looked at the time. Midnight, again! Good thing she'd gone to bed early. Stomping down her hallway, she didn't grab any of her weapons, since this midnight pounding thing was getting old. Once she got to the basement, she entered the underground room through the fireplace door, walked over to the door leading to the underground streets, and threw the door open.

Mavis, Lulu, and Delight giggled when they saw Granny in her sexy nightie.

"We didn't know Franklin was was with you!" Delight said, blushing.

"We wouldn't have disturbed you if we did," Lulu blurted out.

Granny, with a confused look on her face said, "Franklin's not here!"

Mavis, Lulu and Delight all dropped their jaws and their eyes became the eyes of hoot owls.

Delight stammered, "Ah, we didn't mean to disturb you and ah, ah, Silas?"

"We won't tell Franklin," Mavis promised.

"Our lips are sealed," Lulu echoed Mavis's promise by making a zipping gesture with hands across her lips.

"Silas isn't here and neither is Franklin. Why would you think that? More importantly, why are *you* here?" Granny asked.

All three of them stared at Granny's nightgown. Granny followed their eyes. "What's the matter with you three? Can't a girl wear what she wants to to bed? Again, why are you here?"

"You have to come with us, Granny. There's a break in the case and we need to figure out what to do with it," Mavis answered.

"Yes, a break." Lulu and Delight nodded.

"It's midnight. You couldn't have told me earlier?" Granny asked.

"We all decided we liked midnight sleuthing," Mavis said as the other two nodded their heads.

"Where's the pastor? Did she chicken out after our last adventure?" Granny asked.

The other three women looked back and forth, giving each other a secret look that Granny missed. "She might join us later," Delight answered.

"Fine. Wait a minute and I'll go and get dressed. But....George and Silas better not be in on this and better not interrupt us this time. Hopefully, you came up with a better cover than last time," Granny warned as she went back into her house to change.

CHAPTER NINETEEN

The only person they saw in the underground streets on their way to their destination was Jack Puffleman, manager of AbStract. He was exiting AbStract through the underground door. He didn't see the women and they were very quiet, making sure they didn't alert him to their presence.

"I wonder what he's doing at AbStract at midnight," Lulu whispered.

"I'm glad he didn't see us," Delight added. "He might have told Franklin we were out and about again. Then you'd be in trouble, Granny."

"This was your idea, not mine. Let's get to the Pink Percolator. I didn't have my donut today and I'm sure you have one for me," Granny remarked.

All three women kept walking, glancing at each other with guilty looks on their faces. They finally stopped at the lift to Graves' Funeral Home.

"Why are we stopping?" Granny asked, "Remember the street is open to your place, Delight."

"We don't want to be disturbed. Delight charmed Gravy into giving us the code to the lift, although he didn't know he was doing it." Lulu shook her head in wonder at how Delight had gotten the information.

Delight giggled at the thought. "I begged him for a ride on the lift. I told him it was like riding the elevator and that I missed elevator rides and this was the only elevator in Fuchsia—well, the riding kind anyway. He took pity on me and took me down the lift. I watched as he punched in the code."

"And George would never think of looking for me in the mortuary," Mavis explained, "He knows I have an aversion to dead bodies, although we seem to have uncovered a few lately. So, we figured we were safe to meet here."

Delight punched the code as they got on the lift. The lift moved up, the floor parted to make room for the lift, and the ladies entered the funeral home. All was dark and quiet.

"I have it on good authority that there are no bodies here at the moment, so we're alone," Delight whispered.

"If we're alone, why are you whispering?" Mavis asked. "There's a table in the back room where we can meet. We can turn the light on and no one will see us."

Mavis led the way through the darkness to the back room where they closed the door and turned on the light.

"Now what?" Granny asked.

"We wait," Mavis answered.

"For what?" Granny asked suspiciously.

A noise could be heard coming from the outside room. It was the lift.

Granny jumped up. "I didn't bring my weapons; my pitchfork is still in the trunk of my car."

No one else seemed alarmed at the sound of the lift.

"What's the matter with you? You can't just sit there. Someone's going to find us and we'll be back at the police station and they'll throw the book at us!" Granny warned.

The others sat quietly and didn't answer Granny.

"Are you daft? We need to hide before Gravy finds us!" Granny cried.

There was a rap on the door and Granny heard a "Are you there? We're here."

Granny gave the others a scathing look and since she was already up, she opened the door. Pastor Henrietta and Amelia entered the room.

"Quick, close the door, Granny! We don't want to be found out," Mavis instructed, getting up herself to close the door.

"What is this, an audition for a sister act?" Granny sarcastically asked her friends.

Pastor Henrietta decided to take the lead. Walking over to Granny, she put her hand on Granny's shoulder and shoved her into the nearest chair. "Sit!"

Turning to Amelia, Pastor Henrietta gently asked, "Amelia, would you please take your place at the table?"

Pastor Henrietta took a seat in between the two sisters. The others sat back quietly, eyeing Granny and Amelia with scared expressions, not sure the room wasn't going to explode with all the tension emanating from Granny and Amelia.

Pastor Henrietta looked pointedly at Granny. "You have a crime to solve, Granny. Between you two sisters, you have the answers. You can't do it separately because you have to put the entire story together so we can follow the clues. The police can't solve the crime unless they know the story. The four of us have decided that it's time that you, Granny, get over your stubbornness, talk to Amelia and let us in on the story so we can help you. We aren't leaving this room until we do so. Right, ladies?"

Lulu and Mavis shook their heads, agreeing with her.

Granny gave Pastor Henrietta a skeptical look. "Who are you and what did you do with sweet Pastor Henrietta?"

Pastor Henrietta gave a small giggle. "I did that well, didn't I? Did I sound stern enough? Granny, my dear," she said, patting Granny's hand. Then, turning to Amelia, she said, "Amelia, my dear," and patted Amelia's hand with her opposite hand. She picked up both their hands and joined them together. "May you join hands in harmony and love for the rest of your lives."

Granny and Amelia glanced at each other, remembering their earlier days. They nodded and at the same time stood up, pulled Pastor Henrietta with them, and brought both arms to her middle. Granny lifted Henrietta's feet up while Amelia pushed her head down, and they flipped her over their arms making her turn a summersault.

"Well, I guess that went well," Pastor Henrietta remarked, steadying herself by leaning on her chair.

The others stood up when the twirling began, not sure whether to rescue Henrietta from Granny and Amelia's clutches, or to run, in case they were next.

"We still have it!" Amelia laughed.

"Yup, used to do that for fun to unsuspecting people, although we almost dropped you, Henrietta," Granny admitted.

Sitting down at the table, the friends waited for Granny and Amelia to tell their story.

"I'm not sure I know the story. All I know is Amelia married my Robert and I was forced to marry her Ferdinand," said Granny.

"Ferdinand was engaged to Amelia?" Delight asked.

"Yes, he was. My parents had decided that he was a good fit for me. He was solid, dependable, and reliable and would provide for me, they said," Amelia explained.

Granny picked up the story. "And I was in love with Robert Blackford. My parents weren't happy about it. They thought he was too spur-of-the-moment. He had no plans for the future. He always used to say, 'The future will take care of itself and it's ours for the taking.' He wanted to take me away on a wild adventure. And I was ready. I was tired of always having to behave a certain way and when I didn't, my parents would look at me with disappointment in their eyes. But behaving was boring."

Amelia nodded, "I was quiet and didn't have the courage that Hermiony did. I secretly admired Hermiony's courage and her sense of adventure. I saw her having an exciting and wild adventure with Robert. Ferdinand was a good man, but there was no place for dreams in Ferdinand's life. Our mother and father were like that too.

"So you stole him, Amelia! You stole him and broke my heart." Granny pounded her hand on the table, making the others jump at the gesture.

"Well, actually, I saved you. And…you should thank me," Amelia said haughtily.

Pastor Henrietta jumped in to soothe the waters. "Now, let's work on feeling peace and love as we all continue this journey into your past."

"Yes, remember, we need to get to the bottom of these murders and you two know more than you know," Delight added.

Amelia looked at Granny, "What did she just say?"

Granny shrugged her shoulders, "Once you get to know her, you'll understand *Delight speak*."

"Back to the story, I'm taking notes for my new reality show, *Milk Toast Versus Wild Child*. Maybe there's a better name for it. I'm afraid everyone might think it's a wrestling match." Mavis was going to go on about her reality show, but Pastor Henrietta held up her hand for everyone else to be silent, nodding to Amelia to continue.

"Hermiony and I always used to change places to tease our boyfriends and our parents. It always worked.

She was able to be meek and mild for a short time, and I was able to act the wild child for a short time. It always worked, but we never did it for very long. Knowing what I know now, it would have been too hard for us to take on each other's characteristics for too long a time." Amelia stopped speaking, her thoughts lost in the past.

"And then I got sick and she stole him," Granny said in an accusatory tone.

Pastor Henrietta put up a hand to indicate Granny needed to let Amelia continue.

Granny's voice was enough to bring Amelia out of her reverie and continue the story. "Ferdinand and I were set to be married in a month. I panicked. I wasn't sure I wanted to marry him, but telling my parents would have done no good. I saw my chance when Hermiony came down with pneumonia. I ran into Robert one night when I was in the hayloft of the barn looking at the stars and wondering what I should do. He thought I was Hermiony. She used to sneak out and meet him in secret because our parents so disapproved of Robert. It was then I knew what I had to do."

Amelia sneaked a peak out of the corner of her eye at her sister. Granny sat silently, a sad expression on her face.

"I put on my Hermiony act and he thought I was you. Hermiony and I always told each other everything in those days so I could answer whatever he asked." Turning to the others, she explained, "We would share our deepest secrets. I knew everything about her relationship with Robert."

Granny looked at her sister and in a sad voice said, "I trusted you with everything that was in me."

"I know you did, but you have to understand how desperate I was. I wasn't as brave as you. I couldn't stand up to mother and father and tell them I didn't want to marry Ferdinand. I didn't have the courage and so I pretended to be you. When Robert asked me to run away with him I said yes. I didn't mean to hurt you, but I was so confused and Robert was so charming."

"And he never found out?" Delight broke in on the story.

"Not for two years," Amelia said sadly.

Granny's brow wrinkled, "Well, I'm confused. How did you marry him if he didn't know you weren't me?"

"We went to Las Vegas and got married in a chapel there." Amelia hesitated, stealing a glance at her sister and then said in a soft voice, "I, ah, signed your name."

Granny stood up. "You signed my name? I was married to Robert Blackford and didn't know it? And then I married Ferdinand Fiddlestadt. I was a bigamist? How could you do that to me?"

Frowning, Pastor Henrietta pulled Granny back down in her chair and shook her head. "I suppose it was possible in those days for that sort of mix-up to happen as there were no computers, and records weren't shared all over the country. There was no reason when they issued your marriage license, Hermiony, for anyone to check."

Amelia was about to continue her story when they heard the lift in the funeral home moving.

CHAPTER TWENTY

The women froze as if playing the childhood game Statue. Granny held up a finger to her lips, indicating they should all be quiet. Mavis moved to the door of the room to make sure it was shut and turned the light off. They could hear Giles Graves and Granny's son-in-law, Butch, talking as the lift stopped. Butch worked for Giles Graves from time to time.

Granny opened the door a tiny crack and closed it again. "They're bringing someone up on the lift," she whispered to the others.

The women all whispered at once, "Who?"

"Are they dead?" Mavis asked with a shaky voice.

Granny turned to the women and shook her head, "It's under a sheet. What's your guess?" The women all started to mumble.

"Quiet!" Granny whispered. They all repeated the word after her. Granny shook her head and hoped Giles and Butch hadn't heard. No one would believe this night gathering wasn't her idea.

Soon they heard the voices of others joining Mr. Graves and Butch in the front room.

"That sounds like Thor and the Tall Guy."

"Shh!" Granny motioned to Pastor Henrietta to be quiet. "We don't want them to find us."

Granny and Mavis put their ears to the door to see if they could hear what was being said. Delight moved quietly across the room and turned the lock on the handle of the door. "They'll have to break the door down," she mouthed to the others in the room, but they couldn't make out what she was trying to convey through her silent words because of the darkness of the room.

Amelia's cell phone pinged. She quickly turned off the sound and picked up the phone to see who was calling. She shuffled her way through the dark room over to Granny and held the phone up for her to see.

Granny frowned and whispered, "It's 2:00 a.m. Why would Thor be calling you at 2:00 a.m.?" They both looked at the closed door.

Amelia began to shake. "Someone's dead and in the next room. Thor's in the next room and he's calling me?" her whisper conveyed the panic she was feeling. "I'm going out there."

"You can't! We'll all get into trouble," Delight warned.

The men talking in the next room moved closer to the door. The women heard the knob turn. "It's locked," they heard the Tall Guy say.

"The key's at home. I must have accidently locked the door to the room when I left," they heard Mr. Graves explain.

"I can't get a hold of Amelia; she's probably sleeping and doesn't hear the phone," Thor concluded.

"Well, there's nothing she can do right now anyway. We know she didn't have anything to do with Justine ending up dead in her chocolate factory. We can talk to her in the morning. We have Lars's statement since he's the one who found her," the Tall Guy told him.

The women listening at the door gave a gasp.

The Tall Guy asked the others, "Did you hear that?"

"Oh, it was probably nothing; this old building has a lot of creaks and groans. Probably all the old ghosts," Giles Graves laughed.

"Well, since ol' Gravy here locked us out of his snack room so we could get some coffee, we'll just head over to the station and grab some there. I don't think there's going to be any rest for us tonight." Thor patted the Tall Guy on the back.

"I have a hardware store to run in the morning," Butch reminded them. "Good luck."

"Gravy, you might as well come on over and have some coffee with us," Thor said to the funeral director, "It'll keep you awake. I imagine your day is going to be just as long as ours."

As the men left the funeral home, Giles Graves's loud voice could be heard asking the Tall Guy if he thought this murder had anything to do with the murders out at Granny's farm.

Granny and the others strained against the back room door to hear his answer.

"Too soon to tell, Giles; we don't even know if Justine's death *was* a murder, but we did find out what killed Robert Blackford. You were a big help in helping us figure out that puzzle."

The women then heard silence. They stepped away from the office door and were quiet until they were sure everyone was gone. Pastor Henrietta turned the light back on.

Silence filled the room as the women were still in shock hearing that Justine, who ran the jewelry counter at AbStract, was dead.

"Now what?" Mavis asked.

"We finish the story," Pastor Henrietta answered.

"Well, we can't stay here. What if Gravy comes back to work with the body?" Granny announced.

Delight in a jittery voice asked, "Didn't you hear Gravy say there were ghosts here?"

"Yup, there's one right in back of you," Granny teased.

Delight jumped and turned around. The others laughed. Delight got the joke and laughed too.

"Why don't we all go over to my house," Amelia suggested. "We can finish the story and when the police come to tell me about Justine, you'll all be there to help me pretend shock."

"That's a great idea. In case George wakes up from the spell I put on him last night and realizes I haven't been home all night, we'll tell him we had a slumber party at your house just like you and Granny used to do."

"Mavis, that's a great idea." Lulu who'd been silent since all this started, chimed in, "We can tell them that we wanted to remind you two of your past so you can go on to your future."

All of the women stared at Lulu with amazed looks on their faces. Pastor Henrietta patted Lulu's cheek, "Such wisdom, my dear; you have grown so much tonight in spirit. You will be truly blessed."

"Yah, and if someone finds out we were here, we'll just tell them we were having a séance in the funeral home and Lulu's spirit found wisdom and channeled itself through Lulu, and it's going to be my next reality show." Mavis smiled at the thought.

Unlocking the door to the office, Granny stuck her head into the dark front room. "All clear." She motioned the others to follow.

"How are we going to get to Amelia's house? She's not on the underground streets." Delight pointed out.

"We can't go out the front door; they might still be on the streets on the way to the police station," Amelia warned.

"Well, we can't go back to my house," Granny told them. "George or Silas or Penelope might see us leave the house."

"We could take the underground streets to the Pink Percolator, but then we'd have to walk to Amelia's, and the Pink Percolator is right down the street from the

Police Station so they might see us." Delight shook her head at another roadblock to getting out of the Funeral Home.

"What if we took the hearse from the garage? The garage opens in the other direction, so they wouldn't see us take it out. We could drive through the back alleys to Rack's and leave the hearse in the parking lot. We could wipe our fingerprints off. Since its dark and the hearse is black, it will be hard for someone to see it, and if they did, they'd think Gravy was having a clandestine meeting with his girlfriend." Amelia realized what she'd just said and started to stammer, "Well, uh, um, someone told me he might have a girlfriend."

"It's clear you don't get subterfuge very well, Amelia," Granny addressed her with a disbelieving tone. "You don't think Thor and the Tall Guy and Franklin would suspect that possibly we took the hearse since we weren't home all night?"

Granny continued, "This is what we're going to do. We're going to go back down to the underground street and we're going to use the hole to the alley that the shysters use to get in and out of the streets. The city didn't close it up because since the shysters are the ones that led us to the underground streets, the officials felt they should be allowed to continue to use it. They widened it a little bit for Baskerville. We should be able to fit through there."

"I get it," Delight commented, excited that she'd caught on to Granny's plan." We sneak down the alley to the next street and take the back alleys to Amelia's."

Mavis reminded them, "Be careful; apparently we have a killer on the loose."

At the word *killer*, Delight and Lulu grabbed each other's hands and shrank back into the room.

"We better go," Granny advised, "Gravy might be back."

Silently, they moved through the front room to the lift.

Lulu hung back. Can't we take a peek at Justine? She was such a nice girl. I can't believe she's dead."

"No, we have to get out of here before we're discovered. And if we get caught looking at Justine in the middle of the night, they might think we killed her and are here to get rid of the evidence." Granny reached out and grabbed Lulu to bring her along with the rest of them.

As the lift reached the underground street and the floor closed up, they heard the latch being opened to the funeral home door. Gravy was back.

CHAPTER TWENTY-ONE

The journey to Amelia's house was smooth. The only things in the back alleys in the middle of the night were the cats and dogs out on their nighttime routines. Fuchsia didn't have a leash law. The entire community embraced each other's pets and watched out for them. If some of the pets got a little unruly, they would talk to their pet parents and the pet parents would take care of it. The one thing the City of Fuchsia did do was to offer free spay and neutering so pet families did not get out of control.

Once safe at Amelia's, the women were jovial because they hadn't been discovered. They were about to sit down at Amelia's kitchen table to hear the rest of the story when Mavis spoke up, "I don't know about you all, but I think I need to sleep; this has been a bit too much reality for me."

"Me too," Lulu agreed.

"Do you have a few couches where we can crash for a couple of hours, Amelia?" Delight looked around for somewhere soft to settle for a few winks.

"Good idea! Then maybe we'll get the story straight and we can plan. I have three bedrooms and I finished the basement and there's a sofa bed down there. Take your pick!" Amelia indicated the basement door as she moved down the hall to her room.

"I'll take the couch up here and stand guard," said Granny as she plopped herself down on the couch that Delight had been eyeing.

"I remember the basement. Granny and I have fond memories of makeovers and the basement window. I want to see what Amelia's done to it, so I'll sleep watch in the basement in case someone comes in through the lake tunnel," Mavis said as she proceeded down the basement steps.

"I'll go with you; there must be room for two on that couch. Do you snore?" Pastor Henrietta asked, following Mavis down the steps.

"I guess we get the two bedrooms, Lulu. See you in a couple of hours. It's almost daylight now," Delight yawned as she and Lulu navigated the hallway to the bedrooms.

Granny lay down on the couch and fluffed the couch pillow. Poor Justine! What had happened to her? Could it have had anything to do with Jack Puffleman coming out of AbStract in the middle of the night? She had died at Amelia's Chocolate Factory so it didn't make sense that Jack Puffleman would have a part in it. Or did it? Granny's eyes closed and she fell asleep with visions of Justine's cold, lifeless, covered body in her head.

The doorbell's ring woke Granny out of her uneasy sleep. She looked around and it appeared no one else had heard the doorbell. She could hear soft snores coming from the other rooms. Glancing at her cell phone as she pulled it out of her pocket, she saw that it was 6:00 a.m. She assumed the Tall Guy and Thor couldn't wait any longer to tell Amelia about what had happened to Justine.

Sitting up from her reclining position, she steadied herself before rising to answer Amelia's door.

Opening the door, she saw the Tall Guy but no Thor. She wondered where her son was—hopefully at the hospital helping his wife have her new grandchild.

"Why, Ephraim! Why are you here so early in the morning?"

"I'm so sorry if I woke you up, Amelia, but I have some bad news. We tried to call you last night but you weren't answering your phone."

"Oh, yes. Well, I was very tired. I had a few friends over and we talked until all hours of the night. We had a little slumber party like we used to do when we were younger, but we're so old we fell asleep around ten. You can hear by the soft snoring that my guests are still here. Just can't party like we used to. Come in, but we should whisper so we don't wake anyone."

The Tall Guy came into the house and Granny gestured for him to sit at Amelia's table. "Can I make you some coffee?" Granny looked over at the counter where Amelia had one of those newfangled, one-cup fast coffee machines. "I need my coffee first thing in the morning." Granny moved to make a cup.

"You're sure a lot like Granny, Amelia; she likes her coffee first thing in the morning too. Thor's on his way over to talk to her."

"Really? You needed to talk to both of us?"

"I'm afraid something has happened at your factory, Amelia. Lars took care of it last night but you need to be told and Lars is still being questioned."

"Questioned about what?"

Footsteps could be heard on the basement stairs. Granny rushed to open the door for Mavis.

"Mavis, the Tall Guy came by to tell me that something happened at my factory last night. Maybe you should wake up the others." Granny winked at Mavis. "Make sure when you go into my bedroom and wake Granny up that you tell her that Thor is looking for her at her house."

Mavis frowned and looked from the Tall Guy to Granny, confused. The frown on her face continued as she put her face close to Granny's and looked closely in her eyes. She hesitated before answering, "Okay,

Amelia, I can do that. Wow, this will make a great reality show. I think I'll call it, *The Ol' Switcheroo.*"

Granny and the Tall Guy watched as Mavis went to wake up the others.

Granny turned back to the Tall Guy. "It's so nice of Granny to share her friends with me. Last night we put the past to rest for a little while so we could have a stroll down memory lane." She gave the Tall Guy a sweet Amelia-type smile.

Before the Tall Guy could respond, Mavis, Delight, Lulu and Amelia could be heard whispering in the hallway.

The words, "I get it; I *get* it." rose above the whispering.

Granny looked at the Tall Guy and explained, "Granny occasionally has a hard time understanding, and she gets confused at times, poor dear."

"Can't a woman get any beauty sleep around here?" Amelia barked in Granny's typical tone as she led the group into the kitchen. She addressed the Tall Guy, "You're interrupting our party—the sleep part of it, at least!". Going over to Granny and giving her a quick hug, she continued, "And you've interrupted the reunion between Amelia and me! She's no crook, but she's okay in my book!"

Granny frowned at Amelia trying to do a Granny rhyme and said, "Yes, well, Granny, it appears something terrible has happened and we need to let this nice detective tell us about it."

Pastor Henrietta, who'd stayed in the basement so she wouldn't be seen, listened with her ear to the door. Mavis and she had agreed that Pastor Henrietta would stay hidden in case the Tall Guy caught on to their sleuthing plan. This way they'd have at least one member of their group incognito.

Amelia, speaking in Granny's voice, made a request. "Amelia, I need to talk to you. Sorry Tall Guy, your bad news has to wait. I need Amelia to help me with my girdle; it's holding too much in and it has to be let out––right now!"

Granny, stood up from the table and said in a sweet Amelia voice, "Of course, you understand, Ephraim, that a tight girdle just doesn't let you breath and we have enough people in Fuchsia who aren't breathing."

The two women hurried down the hallway into Amelia's bedroom before the Tall Guy could say a word. Loud whispers could be heard coming from the room, but none of the listeners could make out any of the words. Soon, Granny and Amelia came out of the room, adjusting their clothes. The real Amelia sat down next to the Tall Guy.

"Now that we have our breathing adjusted, please tell me what it is that happened," Amelia smiled at the Tall Guy and reached out and touched his arm.

Mavis, Delight and Lulu looked from Amelia to Granny, who was now sitting next to Mavis. Mavis turned and peered into Granny's eyes. She said to the others, "Guess my next reality show is going to be called *Unswitched*."

The Tall Guy gave Mavis a confused look before telling the women what happened.

"Amelia, your manager, Lars, for some reason, went back to your factory around 12:15 a.m. last night. When he got there, he noticed footprints of chocolate on the floor leading from the vat that heats and stirs the chocolate."

"Yes." Amelia nodded. "The factory is not running yet, but we tested the machines yesterday and that was one of them. We were going to test it again tomorrow. We left the chocolate in there to finish the test."

The Tall Guy nodded his head in understanding as he continued, "When Lars got to the vat, he found Justine's body lying just outside. She apparently had fallen into the chocolate and then someone had pulled her out and left her there. She was dead."

"Poor Lars. I'd better find my stepson. He's bound to be very upset." Amelia started to get up, but the Tall Guy stopped her. "There's more! This wasn't an accident, Amelia. We think she fell into the vat after someone," and here the Tall Guy looked at Granny before continuing, "forked her with a pitchfork! She had tine marks from a pitchfork on her arm and a pitchfork was lying next to her body."

Granny stood up. "And you're looking at me, why? Because I happened to accidently fork the love of my life the other day? I have an alibi for that!"

"Do you own a pink pitchfork, Granny?" the Tall Guy questioned.

"Yes. It's at home in the trunk of my car."

The Tall Guy's phone rang. He looked at Granny as he spoke into his phone, "No, I know she's not home because she's here." He hesitated, listening to the voice on the other end of the line. "Claims they had a slumber party and they made up. Says her pitchfork is in the trunk of her car. Thanks." The Tall Guy hung up his phone. "That was Thor. He's at your house."

Pastor Henrietta, after hearing the conversation, decided that it was a good time to reveal herself. The door of the basement flew open. This so surprised the Tall Guy as he was leaning back in his chair, that he lost his balance and tumbled to the floor.

"Oh, my, Ephraim! I'm so sorry I startled you! Are you falling for me just like Granny fell for Franklin?" Henrietta giggled, helping him up from the floor.

The others did what they could to hide their mirth. Delight took a quick sip of the Tall Guy's coffee. Lulu pretended a sneeze and Mavis coughed to hide her giggle.

Granny wasn't so delicate. "When I fall, I do it more gracefully; it's called Granny gravitating. That was more like man overboard!"

"Pastor Henrietta, where did you come from?" the Tall Guy looked at her suspiciously.

"Oh, these poor women—two sisters—at odds with one another all these years, they called me to pray with them and bring peace to their hearts." She nodded her head. "Yes, miracles happen. I was so deep in sleep from all the praying last night that I didn't hear you arrive."

Pastor Henrietta turned to the women. She reached over and took Granny's hand and then with her other hand drew Amelia close to her on her other side. "Do you need these women for anything else? I see they've had a shock and I'd like some time alone with them to counsel them. Would that be appropriate? Then I'll bring Granny home."

The Tall Guy nodded his head. "All right, I'll give you time since you're a pastor and all that, but you need to drop Amelia and Granny off at the police station again! I'll tell Thor to meet us there. Don't be long!"

"Can't wait!" Granny yelled to his back as he walked out the door.

Mavis walked over to Granny, grabbed her by the shoulders and looked her straight in the eye. The others watched Mavis, all except for Amelia whose eyes began to twinkle. "Are you the real Granny or are you Amelia?"

"Why you pretended to be me, Hermiony, when you answered the door, I have no idea," the twinkling eyes Amelia scolded.

Granny shrugged her shoulders. "I wanted to find out what was going on and you always used to tell me sugar will get me further than vinegar so I decided to be you, but Mavis decided she needed an early reality show and popped up from the basement before I could get my answers."

Granny paced the floor as the others watched. "We need a plan and we have to finish our story. They may all be connected."

"But why Justine?" Amelia wondered, "She was such a nice girl."

"And why was she at the chocolate factory?" Lulu asked.

"Well, she liked chocolate," Delight giggled, "She had quite the sweet tooth. In fact, she bought some ice cream to take home for someone special in her life. She was pretty excited.

At that moment, Pastor Henrietta's phone played *Amazing Grace*. She looked at the caller id and raised her eyes to the others in the room. "Yes, yes, we're on our way. Yes, I can do that. I'll be sure to bring them all." She hung up her phone and said, "You're all in trouble!"

CHAPTER TWENTY-TWO

Not only were George, Franklin, and Ella waiting for the women at the police station, but so were reporters from the *Fuchsia Flash* newspaper. The reporters brought along their photographers. A couple of policemen were waiting to escort the women into the station and protect them from the reporters.

"My, that was fun!" Mavis remarked. She hadn't been able to resist flashing a few poses for the reporters as if she were a real reality star.

"Why were they here?" Granny asked Thor who was waiting for her inside the door.

"They heard about Justine's death at the factory last night, along with the deaths at the farm and that all the deaths were connected to Amelia."

Granny frowned. "And that's big news? Usually our local newspapers don't publish much murder and mayhem. They like to keep our town pink and perky. They feel gruesome things are the cops' business."

The Tall Guy joined them to escort Granny and her friends further back into the building. "Apparently," he said to her as they walked, "your sister Amelia is quite famous when it comes to business. Amelia Blackford is a name to be reckoned with. You didn't know that?"

Pastor Henrietta saved Granny from answering, stopping the group and saying, "I'm leaving, Granny. If you need any pastoral support, please call me. I'd be happy to counsel you some more." Henrietta then turned to the Tall Guy and said, "And if you need my services helping out with this situation, I'll be at the church preparing for Justine's funeral."

"Where's the pastor going?" Granny demanded to know.

"Home, why?" Thor questioned.

"Why are the rest of us still here and she gets to go home?" Granny asked.

Lulu interrupted the conversation by touching Granny's arm, "I'll talk to you later, Granny. I must get my quilt shop opened."

Granny watched Lulu walk out the door. "She gets to go home too?" Turning around, she saw George and Ella talking to two police officers while Mavis and Delight could be seen through the glass of Thor's office being questioned. Amelia was nowhere in sight.

"Let's go talk in my office, Hermiony." The Tall Guy motioned for Granny to proceed him down the hallway.

"You didn't answer my question," Granny insisted.

"Mom," Thor said, "Mavis and Delight are here because George and Ella reported them missing."

Granny frowned. "Missing? They weren't missing. They were with all of us."

"Well, Mom, it's not usual for them to stay out all night. In fact, the only other time it's happened was when we had them here for questioning and we called their families then." Thor's exasperated tone made it evident that he was frustrated with his mother.

When they reached the Tall Guy's office, Thor indicated to his mother that she should sit down. "Why am I here? I was just at a slumber party; nothing interesting there."

The Tall Guy glanced at Thor and said, "Do you want to tell her or should I?"

Thor ran a hand across his eyes before looking at his mother. "Mom, your pitchfork was found at the scene of the crime."

Granny shook her head. "I told you the last time I saw my pitchfork was in the trunk of my car."

"Your car was also seen earlier parked at the chocolate factory," the Tall Guy informed her.

Granny stood up abruptly. "Impossible! I was home all night after Franklin dropped me off!"

Thor shook his head. "Except when you weren't. What time did your *so-called* party start?"

"Midnight was when they picked me up."

"Justine was killed before midnight," the Tall Guy informed her.

"I want my lawyer."

"You don't have one, Mom. We're just asking you a few questions."

The door to the Tall Guy's office opened and Silas and an unknown man entered the room. "What do I have to do, lock you up so I don't have to keep bailing you out of jail, Mrs. Persnickulous?" Silas asked when he saw Granny.

Granny's brow wrinkled. "Are you talking to me, Silas? And what are you doing here and who's that?"

"It's my new name for you. The situations you get yourself into are ridiculous and—you're a difficult persnickety woman."

Nodding to the stranger, she asked, "And this disheveled person you have with you is who?"

"I can introduce myself." Turning to Thor and the Tall Guy, the stranger continued, "Are you going to charge her? Otherwise, I demand you release her." He pounded his fist on the table so hard the table shook.

Granny, Thor and the Tall Guy jumped at the force and noise of his fist on the table.

Silas, a gleam in his eye, said, "Gentlemen, I'd like to introduce you to Humboldt Thaddeus Archibald Notorious, Granny's new lawyer."

"I don't have a lawyer," Granny stated loudly.

"She doesn't need a lawyer," Thor said calmly, "Do you think I'd let my own mother answer questions if she needed a lawyer?"

"Dad," the Tall Guy addressed the other man, "Why are you here?"

Seeing that the conversation in the room was going nowhere, Granny grabbed a chair, stepped up on it and then climbed on the metal desk in the room. Lifting her foot, she brought it back down as hard as a 100-pound lady could. The thump on the metal silenced the men.

"Now, ask your questions! I have nothing to hide. I did not drive my car last night. After Franklin took me home, I went to sleep. The girls picked me up at midnight. We went to Amelia's (Granny had her fingers crossed behind her at that little lie) and you found me there this morning."

Granny then got down from the table and added one more thing, "Is that what you wanted to know?"

Humboldt Notorious moved next to Granny and pronounced, "My client has spoken."

"I'm not your client," she said.

"Silas's lady has spoken," Humboldt Notorious announced.

"I'm not his lady," Granny declared.

At that moment, Franklin Gatsby knocked and walked in. "Amelia's ready to go. Have you finished with Granny?" Turning to Silas, he asked, "What are you doing here?" Seeing Humboldt, he questioned, "And who are you?"

Hearing Franklin mention Amelia, Granny asked, "How do you know Amelia is ready to go, Franklin?"

"She called me to come down here and get you both. I just talked to her. I stayed while they were questioning her in case they crossed the line and she needed a lawyer. In spite of her worldly company, she is unsure of herself; her second husband handled most of the technical details for her company."

Granny gave Franklin a suspicious look. "And my fiancé would know this how?"

Franklin ignored Granny's question and turned again to Humboldt Notorious. "Again, who are you?"

Granny piped up. "He's my lawyer! Silas hired him. We have to be going now if you're done with me, Thor. Silas will give me a ride home; it's on his way."

Silas laughed and turned to the Tall Guy, "Can I take Mrs. Persnickulous home now?"

"In a minute; you all need to clear out including you, Mr. Notorious; I need to talk to my mother as her son," Thor instructed, opening the door to usher everyone out.

Humboldt warned before leaving the room, "My client will let me know if you cross the line. No shenanigans. I know how you police work. You badger weak old ladies and break them down bit by bit until they confess and then you lock them up and throw away the key. That's not going to happen to my client, do you understand?" he stated in a loud booming voice.

Granny upon hearing the *weak old lady* bit moved quickly to the door and poked the lawyer in the chest with her finger. "Bolty, enough! You're lucky this is my finger and not my knitting needle or you'd be skewered to the wall so the police could torture you." Granny kept tapping him with her finger as her voice grew louder. "You want weak, I'll show you weak!" and she stomped on his toe with all her weight, although she thought it was lucky she had her high-top sneakers on instead of her pointy heals that she wore when she was an undercover wedding guest.

Turning to the others, she said, "Don't mess with my lawyer." With a smug grin, she sat down in the chair by the desk waiting to hear what Thor had to say.

Thor closed the door and sat down behind the Tall Guy's desk. "We got the autopsy back on Robert Blackford, Mom."

Granny leaned forward in her chair, "And?"

"He died of a heart attack."

"A heart attack? He wasn't knifed like that Dickey Lee Hatchet?"

"No."

"But he was covered with hay and straw?"

"We think whoever killed Dickey Lee Hatchet found Blackford's body and covered it up so it wouldn't be found, just in case it led to the discovery of Dickey Lee's body."

"That was bad planning on their part," Granny said sarcastically.

"What about the reason they were there in the silo in the first place? And where is Amelia's son? Do you know anything?"

"We think they'd come here looking for Amelia's son. They might have thought Amelia knew where he was. They might have thought Lars was Robert's son."

"But why wouldn't Robert know where his son was if he stole his son all those years ago from Amelia?"

"We're working on that and you are *not* to stick your nose in it. Leave this to us, Mom! Do you understand? And why was your car at the factory?"

"Where's my lawyer? You suspect your own mother! Did you ever think that maybe Gram Gramstead is behind all this? Maybe she got out of jail! Maybe she's back! This is her MO, you know."

Thor shook his head in exasperation. "You're fixated on Gram, Mom. She's long gone. Maybe you drove your car to Amelia's factory and you just don't remember."

Granny decided to play along. "Hmmm. I did forget my dentures at home the other day. I'm so lucky we have Mr. Pigster now. He brought them back to me. He tried to fit them into Baskerville's mouth at first, but Baskerville still has his teeth. Did someone say I had a ride home?"

CHAPTER TWENTY-THREE

Granny walked out the door of the police station with Silas, just as Amelia was getting into Franklin's car. "Look! They're just perfect for each other; he's the honey to her milk toast," Silas remarked.

Ignoring Silas's remark about her fiancé and her sister, Granny grudgingly got the words out that she knew she needed to say, "I suppose I should thank you, Silas, for hiring me a lawyer."

Silas leaned in close to Granny, looking around to make sure no one else was in hearing distance. "I have a confession to make; he's not really a lawyer. He's an ex-cop friend of mine from Alaska who happens to be in town. His nickname is Snowshoe."

Granny jumped back away from Silas. "You hired me a fake lawyer? What's the matter with you? You really want me in the hoosegow, don't you? You hired someone who can't get me off the hook—on purpose? You want me going down for this?" Granny's voice got louder with each word. People inside the police station, including Thor, were about to come out to see what had upset Granny when Silas grabbed her and hustled her into the passenger side of the car. He quickly got in the driver's seat and drove away before they could be questioned.

"What's the matter with you?" Silas barked out the words, "It worked, didn't it? I couldn't see any reason to spend money on a real lawyer when Snowshoe was willing to do it for a favor."

Granny mumbled something under her breath that Silas couldn't understand. She turned to Silas and asked, "Can you drop me off at the Pink Percolator?" ignoring his remark about her fiancé and her sister.

"I think I'll stop with you. I have something to show you when you get home."

Granny didn't hear the comment because she was deep in thought about what Thor had told her. It was almost dinner time which meant it was almost 12:00 noon. Dinner was noon in Fuchsia and supper was at night.

Granny was brought out of her daydreaming by a click of Silas's fingers in front of her face. They could see through the window of the Pink Percolator that Delight and her daughter Ella were having some sort of argument.

"Looks like it's Ella's turn to be worried," said Granny as she observed the scene. "Delight has certainly had her sleepless night worrying about Ella not being at home. At Christmas time, Ella went to visit her boyfriend but didn't tell her mother where that visit would take place or with whom." Granny smiled. "Yup. Ella's getting a taste of her own medicine."

Silas got out of the car, circled around the front, stopped by Granny's door and opened it for her. Granny looked skeptically at Silas and the open door, contemplating his gesture. "I'm not that weak that I can't open my own door. Has your lawyer got you brainwashed with that *weak old woman* idea he has in his head about his older clients?"

Silas raised his eyebrows and made a sweeping gesture with his arm. "I'm wooing you, Hermiony Vidalia Criony Fiddlestadt."

"Well, woo hoo!" Granny answered. "What do you want, Silas? I'm already taken."

Silas chuckled as he again held a door open for Granny, this time, the door to the Pink Percolator. "Wouldn't you rather have horseradish over honey?"

Delight bustled to the door to greet Granny. "What did the police want, Granny? Did they handcuff you? What did you tell them?"

Granny winked at Delight so that Silas didn't see. "Delight, we need some refreshment. Let's talk about something more pleasant." Granny sat down at the nearest table. Silas followed her lead.

"Okay, I'll get you some specialty Boneyard Coffee and a Grannylicious Chocolate Fudge Whipped Cream Fluffy Nut." Delight turned to Silas, "Same for you?"

"Why not? I like to live dangerously."

The front door opened and Amelia and Franklin walked in. Seeing Granny and Silas, they waved and came over to the table. Amelia gave Granny a piercing look. "Hermiony, what did you say at the police station? Did you tell them that we were at my house all night?"

With an innocent air, Granny answered for Franklin's and Silas's benefit. "Well, yes, Amelia. We have nothing to hide, right?"

Delight called from the kitchen, "Granny could I see your for a minute? I need to check on a topping for your dessert."

Granny left the table to join Delight in the kitchen as Franklin and Silas were debating where the shysters and the cohorts had been during the night. Amelia raptly listened to their conversation.

"What is it, Delight?" asked Granny.

"Could you check on Ditty Belle? She didn't come with us last night and the receiver at Persnickety's Book Store must be off the hook. Her cell phone goes straight to voice mail. Or…have you heard from her?"

"Keep those guys busy out there, Delight," said Granny, "and I'll sneak out and check on her. In fact, I'll walk home. I'll be there before they know it. I need to do some thinking about this entire mess."

Granny snuck out the side door of the patio. It was a block or so to the book store. On her way past the Ecstatic Emporium, she noticed a big barbeque fork in the window of the kitchen store. She popped in the door and hollered back to Hotdish Herringbone who was the owner of the store. Hotdish was the nickname for Hazel Herringbone. She'd gotten the nickname not because she loved to cook and make hot dishes, but because she was good-looking, and thus the name, hot dish. Hazel didn't mind and took the joke about her name with a laugh.

"Hotdish, send me a bill for this fork."

"Will do, Granny, ya going to do some barbequing?"

"You never know what you might run into that needs a fork. Some things are just too hot to handle."

Granny had no need any more to walk slowly since her undercover days were over. The treadmill in her basement kept her old legs moving. Taking the back way through the alley, she moved quickly, finally arriving at the back door of Persnickety's. The door was unlocked and Granny entered the bookstore. It was unusual for the door to be unlocked if Ditty Belle wasn't open for business. She steadied her new BBQ fork in front of her as she called to Ditty Belle.

"Up here, Granny!" Ditty Belle answered from the front of the store.

Granny carefully entered the front of the store, but it was dark and empty. She tightened her grip on the fork.

"Where are you?"

"Up here."

Persnickety's Bookstore was an unusual building. Ditty Belle had remodeled it by taking out the upstairs floor and leaving part of the floor as a loft on one end of the building. The rest of the store had high ceilings reaching into a glass wall and glass-domed ceiling at the front of the shop. Bookshelves lined the walls all the way up to the ceiling except on the end with the dome. If one needed a book from one of the top shelves, they used the tall movable ladder to reach the shelves. The top shelf was standing height near the ceiling level and was left empty and used as a walkway to the domed glass that ended at a loft so that at night, Ditty Belle and her friends, or special customers, could climb up and look at the stars or look down upon the streets through the dome.

Granny looked up to where she heard Ditty Belle say "Up here." Sure enough, Ditty Belle was on the top level in the loft surrounded by the glass dome. Granny lowered her fork.

"What are you doing up there and why aren't you answering your phone?"

"I spent the night up here."

"We spent the night at Amelia's and the morning at the police station. You should have been with us. Can't believe you missed all that fun because you stayed here reading."

"Why were you at the police station?"

"Long story, why are you still up there?"

Ditty Belle pointed to the floor. "You do need new glasses or your eyes are older than you are."

Granny looked down at where she was pointing and saw that the long ladder that had fallen to the floor. With a glimmer of mischief in her eye, Granny turned toward the door. "Hmm, don't see a thing. Well, have fun reading. I'm sure I'm supposed to be home by now."

"Wait! Get me down!" Ditty Belle pleaded. "I have some information. That's why I'm up here in the first place. I was calling you when I dropped my phone."

Granny set her fork down and picked up the ladder, propping it up with the hook catching the top shelves. Granny put her foot on the first rung of the ladder. "I'm coming up. I want to see what it looks like from up there."

Ditty Belle moved over onto the seat under the domed skylight.

Granny plopped herself down next to Ditty Belle and looked down. "Quite the view you got up here. This would be a good place to drop the paper snow that we shower the town with during Polar Bear Days. Do any of the windows on the side of the dome open?"

"Yup; great idea. I'll pass that along to the committee." Ditty Belle shook her head in agreement.

"Didn't you have any customers this morning? Why didn't they find you?" Granny asked.

"The front door is locked and no one thought to check the back door and the lights were out," Ditty Belle explained.

"So what is the news?"

"I knew we had a book in here that listed all the families in Fuchsia back in the days when you were growing up, Granny—even the ones in the country. Here it is. I found it. I got so excited at what I'd found in the book when I crawled up here to read it, that I accidently kicked the ladder off the shelf and it fell to the ground."

"Tell me what it says since my eyes are older than I am," Granny snapped.

"Well, it appears that the Blackford family did live in Fuchsia. When they were here they had two children, one of whom was Robert. The family moved out of town when Robert was eighteen. Robert stayed behind.

Wasn't it wonderful that back then the town kept track of its citizens? We should write a book just like this about the good citizens of Fuchsia today," Ditty Belle suggested, "although, I don't think anyone knows this book exists or they would have known about Mrs. Shrill."

"Why don't I remember who Robert's relatives were?" Granny wondered aloud. "Maybe Amelia knows. He told me his parents were gone. I thought he meant dead and I was eighteen and I didn't want to think about that."

Ditty Belle frowned. "Didn't you wonder where he lived?"

"He was an older man, at least two years older than me. He told me he had an apartment over in Allure and I had no reason to doubt that. I asked to see it once but he told me it wouldn't be proper. That was before my proper days and I didn't care about proper, but I let it go. I thought it was a strange remark for someone so free and loose." Granny's voice trailed off as she thought back to the days when she was with Robert.

The back door slammed, "Granny! Ditty Belle!" Silas's voice could be heard from their perch.

Granny grabbed Ditty Belle's arm and put a finger to her lips, motioning Ditty Belle to be quiet. She motioned they should both lay flat on the loft so Silas couldn't see them from down below.

Ditty Belle mouthed the word, "Why?" to Granny, but Granny just shook her head.

Silas looked around the bookstore, glancing once up at the loft but not seeing Ditty Belle or Granny. He picked up his cell phone and punched a number. "She's not here. Ditty Belle is missing too. The back door was unlocked. You'd better call Franklin. He's keeping watch on Amelia. Granny and Amelia have no idea their lives may be in danger. Maybe we should tell them so they will at least let us keep an eye on them. I'll keep looking; hopefully, they aren't really missing." Silas hung up his phone, took another glance around and left by the back door.

Granny and Ditty Belle sat up. Ditty Belle grabbed Granny's arm. "Someone's trying to kill you."

Granny shook off Ditty Belle's arm. "No, he said my life was in danger. There's a difference. He didn't use the word *kill*. It could mean I drive too fast or—I'm not getting enough exercise and going to have a heart attack or—my kids are going to put me in the wrinkle farm. I didn't hear the word *kill* and neither did you."

CHAPTER TWENTY-FOUR

Ditty Belle let Granny out of the back door of Persnickety's Bookstore before going back to the front and unlocking the door to open her business for the day. Granny made sure the coast was clear before she left the building. She strolled out of the alley to the street and began her walk home, stopping by AbStract on the way.

Jack Puffleman himself was behind the jewelry counter. "Granny, Silas Crickett and the Tall Guy are looking for you."

"A gal can't even shop without the men in this town trying to stop her from spending her hard earned money."

"Well, they said I should call them if I saw you." He started to pick up his store phone.

Granny still had the fork she'd bought from the Ecstatic Emporium which she'd made sure not to leave Persnickety's. You never knew when it might come in handy. Raising the fork, she gave Jack a little poke. It was enough to make him drop the phone.

"Ouch! Why did you fork me?" the AbStract owner whined.

"Just so we're clear, Jack Puffleman. I don't tell the police what you were doing coming out of AbStract at midnight on the night Justine was killed, and you don't tell my kids that I'm here now."

"You don't think I killed Justine?" he asked.

"Did you?" Granny held the fork in front of her, threatening him with another stab.

"Why would I kill Justine? I loved her." Realizing what he'd just said, he backtracked. "I mean I loved her like a daughter."

Granny screwed up her face and made a disbelieving sound.

"No, really, Granny. I would never have hurt her. I did see her that night though. We met right here. She said she had something to tell me. She's my daughter."

"Puffy, can't you come up with a better alibi than the old I-just-found-my-daughter routine?"

"She told me that night and now she's dead." Jack Puffleman put his head in his hands, sobbing as he spoke, "She's been working for me the past few years and I never knew she was my daughter. She just found out herself. We wasted so much time because we didn't know."

"Do the police know?"

"No, I haven't told anyone but you. And Granny, no offense, if you tell anyone they'll think it's just the ranting of your imagination. My wife and family don't know I was married before. Justine's mother never told me about her, and I see no reason now that she's dead to tell them."

Granny shook her head. "I'm going now, Jack. Remember our pact. You don't call Silas and the Tall Guy, and I don't tell your secret."

Jack Puffleman wiped his brow at Granny's words and nodded his head. He didn't hear Granny's last words as she left his building, "For now."

Granny walked slowly, making sure not to step on the cracks of the sidewalk. She still held on to her superstition of the little ditty she'd learned during her childhood. She always enjoyed the walk, though she did miss the exchanges that she and Mrs. Shrill used to have every time Granny walked by her house.

Angel was in the front yard of Mrs. Shrill's old house playing with Baskerville and Mr. Porkster. It looked like the pot belly pig might be here to stay. Thor and Heather, along with Angel, now lived in Mrs. Shrill's old house.

"Granny, Granny, you're here!" Angel jumped in excitement.

"I'm on my way home."

Angel's face puckered up in a thoughtful expression. "Granny, I thought you were lost."

"Lost? Angel, when have you ever known me to be lost?" Granny asked.

Angel thought for a moment, "Well, your cars have been lost, and you've been kidnapped, so that's kind of like being lost."

"Why did you think I was lost?"

"Cause my dad, Thor, said he had to keep an eye on you so you didn't disappear. Then they couldn't find you, so I thought you were lost. But I suppose a magician could make you disappear. Is that what happened? A magician made you disappear so they couldn't see you?" Angel whispered the last sentence, looking around to make sure no one heard.

Granny laughed. "How is your mom, Angel?"

"She's resting. She says the new baby needs to rest because he kicked up a storm last night, but I didn't see a storm, did you, Granny?"

A car pulled up alongside the curb where Granny and Angel were talking. "Angel, could I borrow your Granny?" Silas Crickett inquired.

"Yes, Grandpa Silas; she's not lost anymore. I found her."

"Grandpa Silas?" Granny's tone was guarded, not wanting to blow her stack in front of her granddaughter.

"Yes," replied the child. "He's going to be my new Grandpa!"

Granny gave Silas a piercing look.

Angel continued her explanation. "Grandpa Franklin said that isn't going to happen unless hell freezes over. I didn't know what that meant, but if Grandpa Franklin said it, then it must be true because he never lies."

"Angel, I think you'd better go in and check on your mom. I have to go somewhere with Silas."

"Okay. Can Baskerville and Mr. Pigster still stay and play?"

"For a little while, but send them home soon," Granny instructed.

Granny watched Angel take the two animals into her house while she checked on her mom. Turning to Silas, she hesitated, walked to the car, opened the passenger door and got in. "Take me to Amelia's."

CHAPTER TWENTY-FIVE

Granny raised her hand to knock on Amelia's door. As her hand was coming down to hit the wooden door, the door opened, and Granny's hand knocked on Amelia's nose.

"Again!" Amelia said, turning to Franklin who was sitting in Amelia's living room, "At least she didn't use an umbrella this time." She motioned Granny and Silas in as she rubbed her nose.

Franklin stood up and came over and shook Silas's hand, "Crickett, good to see you."

Granny stepped back at the congenial welcome Franklin gave Silas. "Gatsby, are you ill? You just shook Silas's hand."

Silas moved closer to Franklin and patted him on the back. "We've decided to bury the hatchet. Not good for the blood pressure, you know."

Granny looked from Franklin to Silas, trying to decide if their friendship was a charade or if she was missing something.

"Isn't it great, Hermiony?" asked Amelia. "Now we can all be friends. I've been talking to Franklin and explaining that it's a waste of energy to hold a grudge." She turned to address Franklin. "Isn't that right, Franklin?"

Silas coughed while Franklin had a look of guilt on his face. "That's right, Amelia. After all, Silas has agreed to take Baskerville, Mrs. Bleaty, and now Mr. Pigster after we're married. The shysters will live with us in my Victorian house."

"What?" Granny yelled. She was about to add to her exclamation when Amelia stepped in and cut off the tirade that was on the tip of Granny's tongue.

"Why are you here, Hermiony?" asked Amelia. "I thought Silas was taking you home to rest. It was very nice of Franklin to come and get us from the police station. I thought he'd be the one you wanted me to call. I knew you'd be too stubborn to call him, but you already had Silas picking you up."

"I didn't call Silas!," cried Granny. "He just showed up with his lawyer, Snowshoe Notorious. Don't you know he's always interrupting my life, but that isn't why I came over here."

Granny indicated that Franklin should sit next to her on Amelia's couch. She cleared her throat. "Um, Franklin, I realized today at the Police Station that life is too short to put things off. Let's set a date for our wedding." Granny leaned over and kissed Franklin on the cheek.

Amelia was quiet as she observed Granny and Franklin together on the couch.

Silas broke the silence. "Great! Now that we have all this sentimental hoo ha taken care of, this taxi's leaving. If you want a ride, Mrs. Persnickulous, you'd better say your good-byes."

Franklin took Granny's hand. "I'll book the church for a day in August, Hermiony. This is just what I've been waiting to hear."

Granny glanced at Franklin and then gave a challenging look in Silas's direction. "I think it's time for me to go home. It's been a long day and night. Franklin can give me a ride."

Franklin hesitated and gave Silas a long look before answering, "I, ah, think I'd better to stay here, Hermiony. I'm meeting someone at Rack's soon. You should go with Silas."

"You—want me—to ride home with Silas?" Granny gave Franklin a confused look.

"He trusts me with his fiancé, don't you, Franklin?" Silas's face broke into a huge grin.

Franklin turned away. "That's what new friends are for," he replied, unable to hide his scowl.

Amelia spoke up, "Don't forget about our quilting class tonight, Hermiony."

Granny wrinkled up her face, perplexed, "Ah, quilting class?"

"Oh, you must have forgotten," Amelia chided. 'Lulu is going to show us how to make that birth certificate quilt. You know, the one that lists when people are born or adopted so they have a keepsake of remembrance." Amelia opened her eyes wide at her sister and nodded her head up and down.

"Quilting, tonight? Well, I guess we're quilting tonight," replied Granny.

Franklin thought for a moment, "Hermiony, you don't quilt."

Granny stuck out her chin, "Well, Franklin Jester Gatsby, I guess you don't know everything about me. And even if I didn't quilt, you can teach an old woman new tricks. Let's go, Mr. Supercilious. I'm on pins and needles to get home."

The drive to Granny's street was silent. Both Silas and Granny were deep in thought. Silas was thinking about Justine's death at the factory and Granny's thoughts were on Franklin and why he was spending so much time at Amelia's house. Apparently, he and Silas were watching Granny and Amelia in secret—at least, that's what Granny had surmised from Silas's phone conversation that she and Ditty Belle had overheard at Persnickety's. But why wasn't Silas watching Amelia? And vice versa? After all, she was the one who was engaged to Franklin.

Silas stopped at the curb in front of Granny's house to let her out of the car. "I'll pick you up at 6:30 to take you to Lulu's Quilt Shop and your night of quilting."

Granny slammed the door and walked around the car, stopping at his open window. "I can drive myself, Silas, that is, if someone hasn't stolen my car."

"I'll pick you up."

"Why are you watching me and why is Franklin watching Amelia? Do you think someone's going to knock us off?"

Silas smiled a wicked smile before answering, "You two are so much fun to watch." He laughed before driving on and parking in his driveway.

Granny took a minute to survey the neighborhood before she went inside her house. She and Amelia would have to figure out who they were supposed to be in danger from. Maybe Mrs. Shrill was back and had her own undercover thing going.

The shysters and the cohorts were not home yet. Granny thought perhaps Baskerville and Mr. Pigster were still playing with Angel. She looked at the time on her phone. It was four o'clock. Her stomach rumbled and she remembered she hadn't had anything to eat all day. Turning back to the door, she opened it and peered out. Silas was still standing by his car in his driveway. He was talking on the phone. She'd have to go out the back door and sneak into the side door of her garage to get her car. She could smell Rack's fried chicken already. Making a quick apology to the chickens in chicken heaven, she decided she'd become a vegetarian next week. For the moment, she'd stay away from pork so she wouldn't hurt Mr. Porkster's feelings.

Slipping out the back door, she made her way to the garage, carefully watching to make sure Silas didn't see her. Once in her garage, she decided to check her car for her pink pitch fork. Could it really have been the murder weapon? It was gone! Who took her pitchfork? She knew it wasn't her since she'd been with her friends all night. She hadn't forgotten that. Who had been in her garage? She looked around carefully, but her rumbling stomach reminded her of the reason she was in her garage in the first place. She hopped into her car, turned the key, hit the garage door opener and backed out straight into the street. Out of the corner of her eye, she saw Silas look up, but before he could do anything, she revved the engine and took off down the street.

The parking lot at Rack's was half full. Granny parked next to a black Escalade that looked amazingly like Franklin's. Once in the restaurant, she saw Franklin and Amelia sitting at her favorite booth. Franklin saw her at the same time that she saw him and he motioned her over to the table. Granny sat down next to Amelia.

"Where's Silas?" Franklin asked, looking back toward the door.

"How am I supposed to know? He dropped me off at home and told me he'd pick me up at 6:30 to take me quilting. I was hungry. Can't a lady eat without Mr. Supercilious watching her every second? And why are you okay with him watching me anyway?"

Amelia's eyes widened and she held her breath as she listened to the exchange between her sister and Franklin.

"Because we agreed that there's a killer on the loose, and it all seems to go back to the two of you. Right now, Thor and Ephraim have their hands full with Justine's murder. They asked if we'd keep you—Hermiony—out of trouble. Silas and I put our differences behind us for a few days. He lives across the street from you, so it's easier for him to keep an eye on you, unless you want to move in with me or have me move in with you before the wedding?" Franklin grinned at the thought.

Granny frowned. "So you moved in with my sister instead?"

Amelia's eyes got wide. "No, Hermiony, I would never do that to you! I would never try and steal Franklin!"

Granny pulled her head back and looked Amelia straight in the eye. "Learned your lesson, huh?"

Gretchen, coming to take their order, broke up the conversation before Amelia could answer. "What would you like Granny? Your usual new healthy vegetarian meal?"

Granny shook her head. "I'm giving up vegetarian food for the summer solstice. I'll have fried chicken, mashed potatoes and gravy and onion rings. I'll skip my chocolate dessert. We'll probably have something when we're quilting."

Gretchen frowned in confusion. "I didn't know it was the summer solstice. I didn't know you were a quilter. I haven't seen you at any of the quilting classes that I attend."

"Yes, well, you'd better get our orders. We don't want to be late for class. Do we, Amelia?"

"I'll have the same as my sister," Amelia said, smacking her lips.

Franklin sighed. "If you can't beat 'em, join 'em. I'll have the same."

Granny's phone cackled, "Watch out! Watch out!" She ignored the ring and turned off the sound.

"Silas?" Franklin asked.

Granny turned to Amelia. "So, did you know Lars was dating Starshine, your niece?"

Amelia looked down at her lap. Her fingers tapped the table nervously. "Yes, he met her accidently in the city. They began dating. I already had sent my detective—rest his poor soul—here to find out if you were still in Fuchsia."

"And you didn't think he should tell her?"

Amelia's face was unreadable, "No, I told him not to tell her. I was looking for my son, and I thought Lars could find out more if he spent some time with Starshine. I thought perhaps Robert had been in touch with you. I didn't think you'd tell me if I asked."

Granny got out of the booth. Gretchen was bringing their meals. "I want mine to go," Granny informed the waitress, as she turned back to confront her sister. "You think I would have kept your son from you? Remember, you're the deceitful one—stealing Robert!" Turning back to Gretchen, she said, "I'll wait for my food up front."

Granny took a few steps and turned back to Franklin, "Don't be fooled by her sweetness; you'll regret it. At least with me, you know where you stand or—don't."

CHAPTER TWENTY-SIX

Granny was almost to her car, her food carry-out in her hand, when she spied someone standing by her car. "I see you found me."

Silas answered, "Not too many red Corvettes in this town."

"Franklin and Amelia are here."

"And?" Silas asked.

"Who do you two think are going to get us this time?"

"That's on a need to know basis, and you don't need to know."

Granny gave Silas a disgusted look. "Now you sound like my son and—that's my line."

Silas laughed. "I learned from the best. Let's go eat your food by the lake and then I'll take you to quilting."

"I have my car."

"I'll bring you back to get it when you get done at Lulu's and follow you home. I'm not letting you out of my sight, or your son and my son will send me back to Alaska. That might be as bad as the wrinkle farm or the hoosegow. Some nasty men there might be very happy if I came back." Silas held the door to the passenger side of his car open for Granny.

Granny hesitated before getting into Silas's car for a ride to Blue Bird Park and the lake.

Once they were settled by a picnic table so Granny could eat her supper, Granny continued her inquisition, trying to find out who Silas was protecting her from.

"Wouldn't it be easier if I knew who I had to watch out for?"

"It would be, but we aren't sure yet. We're waiting for some information to come in and then we'll know more."

"So where's your fake lawyer friend?"

"He's staying with me but he's out of town tonight doing a little investigating."

"If he's staying with you, why haven't any of us in the neighborhood seen him?"

Silas leaned across the table, looked around as if checking to see if anyone was listening and then in a soft voice said, "Because he's really a ghost. You only imagined you saw him."

Granny threw a chicken bone at Silas. "You're lucky I don't have my pitchfork."

Silas started to answer when a goose jumped up on the picnic table and snatched the chicken bone that Silas had caught, right out of Silas's hands. In doing so, the goose brushed against Silas and knocked him backward off the bench. All of a sudden barking and meowing filled the air and the shysters bounded up to Silas and plopped on top of him. Furball began licking his hair, while Little White Poodle and Tank ran after the goose. Fish grabbed the bone the goose had dropped and carried it away.

Granny took out her cell phone and clicked a picture. "Perfect photo for the *Fuchsia Flash*. I can see the headlines now, "Cat Saves Crickett from Goose and the Fish Ran Away with the Bone." Get up, Crickett; it's time for me to needle something."

Silas picked Furball off his head. "Maybe after I drop you off, I should take Furball home; the rest of the shysters seem to have left."

Granny pointed to Silas's car. "I think they all want a ride; the others are waiting by your car."

Furball wiggled out of Silas's arms and ran to the rest of the shysters who were trying to jump in the open window of the car.

"I guess we're all going for a ride," Silas remarked while driving the car away from the lake.

"I haven't see Radish lately. Usually she and Baskerville and Mrs. Bleaty are inseparable," Granny said, thinking the animals were a safe topic for the short ride to the quilt shop.

"I think Radish has his tail in a whirl since Mr. Pigster showed up," said Silas. He doesn't quite have the oink down yet and he's embarrassed."

"An embarrassed bird," Granny hooted. "You can tell this how?"

"Every time Radish tries to imitate Mr. Pigster and fails, his feathers droop."

"Well, I guess you'll just have to rename him Droopy Drawers," Granny said sarcastically as the car pulled up in front of Lulu's.

The minute Granny opened her door, the shysters jumped in the front seat, over Granny's lap and out the door. "Something I said?" Granny yelled after them as they ran down the street.

Silas opened his door to follow Granny into the quilt shop.

"You going somewhere, Silas?" Granny raised her eyebrows and gave him look that said *Stop right there*!

Franklin and Amelia pulled up behind Silas's car. Amelia got out of the car and walked up to Granny. "Hermiony, are you over your snitty?" she asked.

"Oh, Amelia, you're so witty," replied Granny.

Both Amelia and Granny burst out laughing, touched hands, turned around, touched feet and said at the same time, "We didn't make a sound."

Baffled, Franklin and Silas looked at each other. "It must be a sister thing," Franklin concluded.

Silas shook his head and in a sing-song voice sang, "Or they could just be ding-ding. Franklin, you and I just made a rhyme." He threw a coin in the air. "On a dime!"

Granny looked at both men. "Don't you want to get back to your feud? You two getting along puts me in a foul mood."

Amelia continued, "Your rhymes are dead, if you keep it up, you'll never be wed." She took Granny's arm and they marched into the quilt shop.

Franklin watched them walk into the quilt shop, arm in arm. "I missed something. When did they make up?"

Silas shook his head and followed the women through the door.

Ditty Belle, Pastor Henrietta, Delight and Lulu were all waiting for Granny and Amelia.

Lulu took one look at Franklin and Silas trailing behind the woman and cut them off before they made it halfway into the store. "Where do you think you're going? This is women only."

"Lulu, we have to stay. It's possible that Granny and Amelia are in danger," Franklin explained.

Mavis joined Lulu. "From who? And it looks like you left George out of this little party of yours. He's going to be upset," she warned.

Silas countered, "George wasn't a cop. We don't want him to get hurt and we can't tell you from who; we aren't sure yet. It's on a need-to-know basis and you don't need to know."

Delight giggled and hollered out from behind the table that was set up for quilting, "That's Granny's line!"

Granny and Amelia sat back to watch the men fend off their friends.

Pastor Henrietta sashayed up to Silas and Franklin, putting her hand on both their arms. "Bless you for wanting Granny and Amelia safe. I commend you for that, but what could happen in a quilt shop? There's safety in numbers, and we'll be protected from above. She gave them both the sweetest smile she could muster before she continued, "We'll be sure to call you when we're done quilting."

Granny picked up some pieces of material. "Yes, when I get done half-cutting, and sewing with a curling stitch that meets the edges and unbinds the fortitude, I'll be sure and call you. It might take a couple of hours though."

George came into the quilt shop just as Granny was finishing her sentence, "Wow that was amazing! I didn't know you knew so much about quilting, Hermiony."

Mavis, taking a sip of coffee, almost choked it back out when George complimented Granny on her knowledge. Raising her eyes to indicate her frustration, she approached George. "And why are you here?"

"I saw the cars and Silas and Franklin walking in the door, so I thought I'd check to make sure nothing was wrong."

"Not a thing," Delight peeped up, "Why don't the three of you go over to the Pink Percolator and wait. Tell Ella it's on the house. Now scoot!" She waved a bolt of material at them.

Franklin planted his feet firmly on the floor in a no nonsense stance. "We think we'll stay."

"Oh, for goodness sake," Granny ranted, "What do you think is going to happen to us in the middle of a quilting session with all of us together? Maybe you should tell us just what you're protecting us from, so we know what or who to look out for. If you'd give me my pitchfork back, I could protect all of us."

Silas approached Franklin. "She's right. Let's go over to the Pink Percolator. They can call us when they're done. After all, who would want to encounter that crabby old woman and her cronies? They'd be more than you could handle, Gatsby." Silas gave Franklin a jab in the arm, indicated to George that he should follow him and walked out the door.

Franklin glanced at the women. "Well, Hermiony, you call us the minute you're done. Got that!"

Meekly Granny answered, "Yes, Franklin, of course."

Amelia took Franklin by the arm and walked with him to the door. "We'll be fine, Franklin." She patted him on the arm as she opened the door and gave him a little push." Once he was through the door, she closed it, watched for a minute to see that he'd joined Silas and George, and then swiftly turned the lock on the door. "Is the back door locked?" she asked.

Lulu nodded.

Granny picked up a sharp quilting needle and pointed it at the women, "Now, what's your point in getting me here? And—wow! We're meeting in the daytime and our watchdogs know where we are. Is this a new strategy?"

"I'm here to finish my story. Perhaps it'll help us find my son," Amelia explained.

Pastor Henrietta added, "Yes, and we want to help you since the Fuchsia Police—no offense, Granny, since your son is co-chief—do not seem to be interested in how it might be connected to the murders."

"Where did I leave off?" Amelia searched her memory.

"Right at the part where you signed *my* name to *your* marriage document, technically making *me* the one who was officially married to Robert. You made me a bigamist! Did you ever get divorced, Amelia? Because if Lars is your stepson, I assume that means you got married again," Granny rasped.

Amelia squirmed in her chair and gave Granny a guilty look. "I, ah, um, no. I could see no reason to file for divorce. How could *I* file for divorce when *you* were the one listed on the marriage license?"

Granny flung her hands in the air in disbelief, "Maybe by forging my name again!"

Pastor Henrietta raised her hand in the air, making a peace sign with her fingers. Both women begrudgingly became silent.

"Go on," Lulu urged.

"I found it hard to keep on pretending to be you, Hermiony. It was in the little things that would show up, but still Robert never suspected. After our son Vitale was born, I decided to quit the act. It was too much, taking care of a baby and trying to be my feisty twin sister."

"Didn't he suspect?" Delight asked.

"Not at first. He put it down to changes after the baby was born, but then he got a letter—I don't know from whom; he wouldn't show it to me. Whoever this person was, I suspect he or she was part of the family he'd never told me about. I kept asking about his family but he told me the memories were too painful to talk about so I respected that. Anyway, this letter had news of Hermiony and Ferdinand and so Robert realized he was married to the wrong sister."

"Well, yah," Granny sarcastically remarked, "You would have thought he'd have figured that out sooner; you were never a very good actress, Amelia, when it came to pretending to be me."

Amelia ignored the outburst and continued, "He said I was an unfit mother because I'd lied and sometime during that night, he left with my son. I never saw them again. I had no money so I couldn't hire an investigator and the police at that time said there was nothing they could do because Robert was Vitale's father."

"So how did you get to be the owner of your renowned chocolate company?" Mavis interrupted Amelia's story.

"I had no money and the only thing I knew how to do was to make chocolate candy. A neighbor felt sorry for me and loaned me a little money to open a small shop. One day, a man named Victor Beddington was traveling through our town and stopped in and tasted my chocolates. He liked them so much he bought 100 boxes of chocolates and took them back to New York. One day, he called and wanted to help me expand; he said his friends loved my chocolates. So, I moved to New York and he helped me start my company. We fell in love and got married. He died a few years ago. I never took his name in case my son ever came looking for me."

Granny was fingering something in her hand that she'd taken out of her pocket as Amelia was talking. "Did this Victor Beddington ever try and find Vitale?"

"Yes," Amelia nodded. "He hired the best private investigators, but they turned up no leads. After he died, I hired a new investigator. He was the one who came here, God rest his soul. He traced a lead back here to Fuchsia, but before he could tell me what he'd found, he was murdered."

Granny stared at the objects in her hand. She reached over and took Amelia's hand, opened it and transferred the objects to Amelia's open hand.

Amelia looked at what her sister had put in her hand and tears began to roll down her cheeks. "These are Vitale's. This is his baby ring and a necklace I bought for him when he was born. Where did you get these?"

"The ring was found at the farm and the necklace was stuck in my door. I think Baskerville brought it home from the farm. I wasn't sure until now that they belonged to your son."

Mavis got up and danced around the table. "She's got the whole world in her hands! She's got the whole wide world in her hands!"

Ditty Belle and Lulu joined in. Soon Pastor Henrietta danced to the back room of the quilt shop and came back, dancing with a pink pitchfork as her partner.

Amelia, still fighting the tears, hugged Hermiony. "These items are my world."

Hermiony hesitated and then scooped Amelia up in a big hug, lifting her to her feet.

"We've got work to do," Granny announced.

Mavis presented Granny with the Pink Pitchfork. "Since the police won't you give you back our last gift to you because they claim its evidence, we bought you a new one. After all, who's going to protect us when we find the murderer and Amelia's son?"

"We need a plan. The watchdogs will be back soon," Amelia warned.

"A plan, no man, a scam, that's our plan," Granny rhymed.

"What?" the women asked, confused by the rhyme.

Amelia translated, "Granny will come up with a plan. It won't involve the men, and we might have to come up with a scam in order to execute her plan."

Wrinkling her brow, trying to understand Granny and Amelia, Pastor Henrietta asked, "How does she know we need a scam if she doesn't know her plan?"

"You got it, Pastor Henrietta, now we'd better head over to the Pink Percolator to find the men before they become suspicious," Amelia suggested.

"Meet in the cemetery tomorrow night at midnight," said Granny to the group in a whisper.

"Uh, Granny," Delight's voice quivered, "Didn't we already have enough cemetery fun last winter?"

"Why, yes, we did Delight; wasn't it fun?" Granny led the way out of Lulu's.

CHAPTER TWENTY-SEVEN

"Weren't we supposed to call Franklin, Silas and George when we were ready to leave instead of meeting them?" Delight inquired, turning to watch Lulu lock the door.

Pastor Henrietta and Mavis turned toward the door and answered Delight at the same time, "Yes, yes, we were."

Granny, stepping off the curb and crossing the street, yelled back, "It's only a few blocks to the Pink Percolator! What do you think is going to happen to us in a few blocks?"

The roar of an engine could be heard around the corner. Granny looked up to see a red '57 Chevy Corvette convertible turning the corner and bearing down on her. Before she could move, the shysters and cohorts galloped out of the alley across the street, attacked Granny, knocking her out of the way of the car and onto the sidewalk. Mrs. Bleaty managed to get her body positioned just right so as to break Granny's fall so she wouldn't hit her head. The car sped away and disappeared.

The women turned around when they heard the commotion and Granny's thump on the sidewalk. They rushed to Granny's side.

"Who am I? Who am I?" Mavis asked Granny, waving a finger in front of Granny's nose.

"How many fingers is Mavis holding up?" Delight asked.

Lulu pulled out a needle from her bag and pricked Granny's ankle right above her foot. "Can you feel that?"

Pastor Henrietta knelt down next to Granny and began praying *The Twenty-Third Psalm*.

Little White Poodle licked Granny's face, Baskerville howled, Furball sat on Granny's chest and purred, Fish pawed Granny's hands, and Tank nuzzled Granny's hair. Mrs. Bleaty who was still sitting underneath Granny's head, rose up and moved Granny into a seated position. "You're a wacky lady!" Granny said, looking at Mavis, "Twenty fingers; don't needle me again, and the person who ran me down is going to need that prayer when I catch up with them."

The women helped Granny to her feet. "Do you know who it was? We were looking the other way? We'd better call Thor and the Tall Guy," Pastor Henrietta suggested.

"It was her! It was her!" cried Granny, "She's back! Gram Gramstead or that evil woman who pretended to be Gram Gramstead is back and she's out to get me. You didn't see that red hair? And she's stolen my car again!"

"We better take her to the ER; she's imagining things," Lulu suggested.

"I'm not imagining things!" Granny yelled at the women before taking off, but the shysters and the cohorts formed a wall in front of her so she couldn't continue on down the sidewalk.

"Where are you going?" Delight asked.

Granny looked at the shysters and cohorts blocking her path and turned around.

"I'm going to find my car and then I'm going to find that woman and put her away for life. Lulu, open up that door; I forgot my new pitchfork. I'm gonna need it." Granny went back to stand in front of the door to the quilt shop, waiting for Lulu to open the door while petting her furry friends. "These guys saved me. They know it's Gram. They have a sixth sense about her."

The women shuffled back into the quilt shop and sat down again at the table they'd just left. Granny sat down too, but not before picking up her pitchfork, tapping it lightly on the floor."

Delight giggled; Granny frowned. "You think there's something funny about this, Delight? You didn't think things were this funny when we were locked in the mausoleum last winter."

"Well, no." Delight tried to hold back her giggles."

Mavis coughed and then giggled. Granny skewered Mavis with her eyes. Then Lulu began to giggle too. Soon Pastor Henrietta let out a loud laugh. "You looked like a gigantic fur coat of many colors lying on the ground with a tiny little goat tail for an earring and a muff for your hands with Mrs. Bleaty under your head and Furball sitting on your chest."

Soon, even Granny was tearing up from laughing so hard. When Silas, Franklin, and George walked in, the women didn't even notice them because they were so involved in making up jokes about Granny's predicament.

"What did we miss?" Franklin asked.

George looked at Mavis. "Mavis, are you telling funny jokes again?"

Granny gave all of the women a stern look.

Pastor Henrietta seeing Granny's look, answered, "We were just discussing the *Twenty-Third Psalm* and someone made the joke that it wouldn't be easy for Granny to lie down in green pastures with all her furry ones; they might get in her way." Henrietta gave Silas and Franklin a sweet smile.

"What kind of blathering are you doing now?" Silas accused. "What are you up to, Mrs. Persnickulous?"

"It's late, after eight, time to get my car, and, no, it's not a date. Time to get to bed, get my books read; tomorrow's another day, so none of you get in my way," Granny rhymed as she opened the door to step outside, taking her new pitchfork with her.

Silas shook his head at Franklin and followed Granny out the door. "I'll take you to your car at Rack's and follow you home."

"I'm walking, thank you." Granny ignored Silas's car.

"Fine, walk. I'll follow you in the car," Silas said to Granny as he got in his car.

Granny peered both ways down the street before crossing it, making sure she didn't miss another near hit from a red Chevy Corvette. She held her pitchfork in front of her just in case.

Silas followed at a slow pace, noticing that Granny was more vigilant than usual while walking past the Fuchsia businesses. She seemed to be checking out the stores and was especially leery of the alleyways before crossing them. The pink pitchfork also gave him a clue that possibly she was looking for someone to fork. He noticed when they arrived at Rack's parking lot, that she gazed at her car for longer than usual before getting into the driver's seat.

Once in her car, Granny looked it over to see if there was any evidence that anyone else had driven her car. She found it the minute she got in. The driver's seat was pushed further back so Granny's tiny feet couldn't reach the pedals. She knew it! Someone had stolen her car and brought it back. Someone was tormenting her and the last person to do that had been Gram Gramstead, but Gram Gramstead was supposed to be in prison.

When Granny and Silas reached their neighborhood, Silas continued on to his driveway while Granny drove into her garage with her red '57 Corvette. Before leaving her car, Granny glanced at the hook on the wall by the side door of the garage. It was empty. Granny scurried out of her car and looked for the spare key for her car on the floor by the door. Had the key fallen down? She checked the other hooks to make sure she hadn't accidently put her spare car keys on another hook. She was digging through the garbage can that was also by the door when the side door of her garage opened and Silas made his appearance.

"Something wrong?" He looked around the garage making sure no one else was there.

"If there was, would I tell you?" Granny snarked.

"I thought perhaps you were waiting for me so we could go up in the turret to gaze at the stars together when it got dark." Silas eyes gleamed with mischief.

Granny pulled her fork out of her car and set the tines firmly on the ground. "I'm looking for something."

"Something you forgot you didn't know?"

Granny gave Silas a confused look.

"Or something that you knew you forgot because you forgot you knew it?"

Granny held her hands up in the air in exasperation, "What are you blabbering about, Mr. Supercilious?"

"Just trying to talk in a language you understand." Silas laughed.

"I'm looking for a key," Granny admitted grudgingly.

"A key?"

"The spare key to my car; it's supposed to be right on that hook." Granny pointed to the empty hook on the wall.

"When did you see it last?"

"When the garage was first built and Franklin brought my car back. I've never needed it."

"And you need it now, why?" Silas inquired. "You just drove your car back home so you have a key."

"Because Gram Gramstead just tried to run me down with my car so she must have stolen my spare key." Granny's voice rose to a high pitch.

Silas was quiet, too quiet. Granny looked at him suspiciously. "Do you know something about this you ornery old coot?"

"Not about this, no."

"Then what?"

Silas took Granny's arm and before she could protest, led her out of the garage. "We're going to my house."

Granny pulled her arm away from Silas. "It's nine o'clock at night; the neighbors will talk. Look, my daughter's outside picking some flowers." Granny wrinkled her nose in thought, "It seems kind of funny with all this hoo-hah that my girls haven't been over here trying to get me to stay out of trouble."

Silas waved to Penelope. "We need to talk and we won't be interrupted at my house."

"Silas, I'm tired. I haven't had much sleep. Remember, I was at a slumber party last night, the police station this afternoon and a quilting party tonight," she said, not telling Silas that she wanted to get a couple hours of sleep before meeting the gals at the cemetery to formulate a plan to find Amelia's son and catch Robert and his brother's killer.

"This can't wait. Remember I told you earlier I had something to show you."

"Fine, I need to make a phone call to Franklin first." Granny followed Silas to his house, glancing to see if Penelope was watching them. Penelope was gone, but Mavis and George were standing in their picture window and smiling. Mavis waved excitedly and pointed to Silas's house making kissing gestures with her lips.

Granny shook her head at Mavis and pointed her pitchfork at Silas behind his back.

Once in the house, Silas poured Granny a glass of wine while Granny moved to the kitchen to make her phone call. "Delight, call the women. We have to postpone our rendezvous until tomorrow night at 12 sharp. Get some shuteye so we'll be bright-eyed and bushy-tailed for tomorrow night," Granny whispered into the phone.

Silas called from the other room, "Tell Franklin to take good care of Amelia."

"Who's that?" Delight questioned, still listening on the other end of the phone.

"Ah, that's Radish; I'm bird sitting for the night. Got to go, Delight; see you tomorrow. Be there or be square." Granny cut the connection.

Silas handed Granny her glass of wine and indicated she should sit down.

"Why am I here, Silas?"

"The person who was masquerading as Gram Gramstead," he began, but Granny stopped him, saying, "Yes, I know; that person is tormenting me again. She tried to kill me and I bet she killed Robert and his brother too. Maybe Dickey Lee Hatchet and Gram met in prison, broke out together, and she killed Dickey Lee, and Robert found them and then she poisoned him to make it look as if he'd had a heart attack." Granny stood up and began to pace. "That's it. We have to tell Thor. That's who you've been protecting me from, Gram Gramstead! But why would she want to hurt Amelia? She doesn't even know Amelia. That's why Franklin is protecting Amelia, isn't it?"

Granny's phone rang right at the end of her tirade. Before Silas could say anything, Granny answered.

"Franklin, I'm so glad you called. I know why you're protecting me. You should have told me but what I don't understand is why you have to protect Amelia."

Granny frowned as Franklin spoke, "Let me talk to Silas, now!"

Silas could hear Franklin's voice through Granny's phone. He took the phone from Granny's hand. "Yes. No. Absolutely not; you know how she is. Right. Never. Exactly. Yes. Did she just call you a few minutes ago?" Silas listened for a second and handed the phone back to Granny.

"Franklin," Granny wasn't able to say anymore before Franklin interrupted her.

"Hermiony, I called because I set the date for our wedding. August 6. How does that sound to you?"

"I say it's about time. August 6. Now, about why you're protecting us." Granny heard the line go dead.

"You weren't calling Franklin when you first got here. Who didn't you want me to know you were calling?"

Granny smiled sweetly at Silas. "What was it you wanted to talk to me about now? Oh, yes; let's get back to our conversation about Gram Gramstead."

Silas paused for a moment and decided to let Granny's unknown phone conversation go. "She's dead."

Granny frowned. "Who's dead?"

"The woman you know as Gram Gramstead is dead."

"She just tried to run me down in my car; she can't be dead. She must be pretending to be dead."

"No, she's dead all right. We all saw the body. Maybe your mind played tricks on you, a flashback, when you saw the car coming at you," Silas suggested.

"It was Gram, I tell you, it was Gram!" Granny saw a flash of red out of the corner of her eye.

"Just call me red!" Humboldt Notorious entered the room with a mop of red hair on the top of his head.

CHAPTER TWENTY-EIGHT

Granny gave Humboldt Notorious a disbelieving look. "You tried to run me down with my car?"

Humboldt looked confused as he pulled the red wig off his head, "No, I found this in Silas's bushes. Thought old Silas here lost it when he was cross dressing last night." Humboldt threw the wig at Silas, laughing at Granny's expression.

"What did you find out?" Silas tossed the wig back to Humboldt.

"When Robert Blackford lived in Alaska he didn't have a son with him. He went by the name of Melborne Shultz."

"Well, if Amelia's detectives couldn't track him and my son couldn't find anything out about him, how did you find him, Snowshoe?" Granny was suspicious of what Humboldt was telling them.

Silas answered Granny's question. "Money talks. I'm not above a little bribery here and there. Apparently, Dickey Lee had plenty of time to talk to his cellmate. When his cellmate was questioned by my son, Ephraim, he said he didn't know anything. But you should know that Dicky Lee happened to be in the same prison where Cornelius is serving time." Cornelius, also known as the Big Guy, previously held the position now held by the Tall Guy.

"The Big Guy is in the same prison as Dickey Lee Hatchet?" Granny shook her head at the coincidence.

"Well, not exactly." Franklin entered the room along with Amelia.

"Amelia, Franklin!" Granny exclaimed, surprised to see them.

"We heard what you were saying as we were coming in the house," Amelia explained. "Why are we here, Franklin?"

"I called them while you were in the other room pretending to call Franklin, Granny," Silas answered, "I figured you were up to no good, so I thought we'd better explain this to Amelia too before you both got yourselves in hot water."

Franklin picked up the story where Silas had left off, "Ephraim and Thor have hit a dead end and they're also up to their ears in Justine's murder. I decided to call in some favors from some of the friends I made while I was a detective in New York. We got the Big Guy transferred to the same prison where Dickey Lee Hatchet was in and guess who his roommate was?"

"How did you get him to talk if Thor and the Tall Guy couldn't?" Amelia asked.

"Like Silas said, money talks. The Big Guy offered Dickey Lee's former roommate a bank account to be waiting for him when he's released from prison next year," Franklin explained.

"Isn't that illegal?" Granny questioned.

"It might be if he actually was going to get the money and be released next year." Franklin chuckled.

Silas smiled. "Yes, Dickey Lee's former roomie sang like Radish, incriminating himself in a case the FBI had been trying to solve for years. Don't know why he spilled everything to Cornelius, but Cornelius turned the information over to the FBI. Because of his help on this, my son is going to be released early. Cornelius will be coming back to live here too at the end of the summer. Of course, he can't go back to his old job, but I think being on the inside of a prison cell instead of putting someone behind bars gave him a real jolt."

"And….we knew how to find out where Robert Blackford had been living so Silas called on Snowshoe here." Franklin nodded at Snowshoe.

"Snowshoe Notorious to the rescue!" Humboldt popped the red wig back on his head before continuing the story.

"I tracked down where Melborne Shultz lived. He was hiding out in the boonies of Alaska. I had to take the mail plane to get to the village where he lived. Apparently, he left a girlfriend there who was none too happy with him. To make a long story short, according to her, he had talked about finding his son. He had gotten into some trouble after he left Amelia, so he gave up his son for adoption and he'd wanted to find his son ever since. When he got a message from his brother Dickey Lee, he left Alaska."

"But if he came back here, he must have thought his son was somewhere here in Fuchsia," Granny said, turning to Amelia, "We're going to find him!"

Amelia, with tears in her eyes, shook her head, "How do we start? That's why I had my detective watching Hermiony. I thought perhaps she was helping Robert hide Vitale somewhere here in Fuchsia. Now I know I was mistaken."

Granny walked up to Amelia and looked her straight in the eye, "I may think you were a fiancé stealer, but I would never keep your son from you. We need a plan."

Franklin held up his hands. "No, you do not need a plan, Hermiony. You and Amelia need to stay out of trouble until we find, I mean, until we solve Justine's and Dickey Lee Hatchet's murders. Thor and Ephraim haven't found the thread that connects the two crimes yet, but since one murder happened at your farm and the other at Amelia's Chocolate Factory, and you two are sisters, we have to assume the murders are tied together."

Granny rolled her eyes. "I can take care of myself." Turning to Humboldt Notorious, she ordered, "Take that ridiculous red wig off your head; it makes me want to hook you like I did that contemptuous woman."

Granny's cell phone rang just as she was going to snatch the red wig off Humboldt's head. Her hand moved from snatch mode to her pocket to grab her cell phone. Seeing it was her new granddaughter Angel, she answered, "Hello, my angelic Angel. What's up?"

"Granny, Momma and Thor said you need to come and meet Herman."

"Who's Herman, dear?"

"He's my new baby brother! We're at the Fuchsia Hospital. And Granny, Thor says he has lungs just like you."

Granny turned away from the other's in the room to hide the emotion in her eyes. "I'll be right there, sweetie."

Angel continued, "Thor said Aunt Penelope would pick you up at your house. Aunt Starshine is coming too. Do you know where Grandpa Franklin is? He isn't answering his phone."

Granny turned and looked at Franklin. "He's right here. We'll meet Aunt Penelope and be right there."

Hanging up her phone, she addressed Franklin, "Where's your phone?"

Frowning, Franklin patted his pockets. "Must have left it at Amelia's."

"Fine detective you are," Granny chided. "We have a new grandson. Do you suppose you can find the hospital without your GPS? Come on! Penelope is waiting for us."

"Wait, wait! I want to go too. I'm a new aunt!" Amelia's voice gave away her excitement.

"You can ride with Franklin," Granny told her, "I don't want to get lost. I'm riding with Penelope."

Granny was out the door before Franklin and Amelia could protest.

"Go on," Silas said to Franklin and Amelia. "Ol' Snowshoe and I will keep digging. With a laugh, Silas added, "Oh, and Franklin, You'd better warn your daughter, now that Granny has a namesake, it'll mean double trouble later on. She'll teach him all she knows."

CHAPTER TWENTY-NINE

Angel was waiting for Granny and Penelope at the door of the hospital. "Where's Grandpa?"

"He's right behind us with Aunt Amelia," Granny answered, taking Angel's hand. "Why don't you lead us to your little brother and mom and dad? Oh, look! Grandpa and Aunt Amelia are here now."

Franklin and Amelia came though the revolving door. "Hello, sweetie!" Franklin greeted his granddaughter.

"I'm going to warn you," said Angel, "he cries a lot. My mom and Thor say he has loud lungs, whatever that is. I'll show you where they are."

Heather was holding Herman, and Thor stood by the bed, mesmerized by his new son when the group entered the room. Seeing them, Heather handed Herman to Thor. Thor took the baby over to his mother. Franklin moved by her side to get a look at his new grandson.

"Mom, Franklin, meet your new grandson, Herman Jester Fiddlestadt."

At the same time, Granny and Franklin remarked, "They named him after me."

Amelia shook her head and couldn't resist. "Yes, poor kid; he doesn't stand a chance."

"Why Aunt Amelia, are you sure you and Granny haven't switched personalities again? That sounds more like a Granny quote," Heather chuckled.

Granny handed the baby to Franklin so he would get a chance to hold his grandson. Turning to Amelia, she said, "Haven't quite got it down yet, Amelia. Good try, no wonder Robert wasn't fooled."

Franklin took the baby over to Amelia and put Herman in her arms.

Amelia looked at the tiny baby and tears formed in her eyes. "I so remember the day that Vitale was put in my arms. In fact, Herman looks a little like him, must be the Criony genes in him."

Granny's eyes were misty when she broke in, "It's late, almost midnight, and we'd better let the new mother get some sleep. Angel, do you want to stay with me?"

"It's okay, Mom, we have a bed for her in this room. It's a family room so we can all bond. We'll take care of her. I heard from the Tall Guy that you've had quite a day. You'd better get some rest too."

"Have you heard any more about Justine and who might have murdered her?" Granny snuck the question in to see if Thor might give her some info in a weak moment, being all misty-eyed at having a new baby.

Thor laughed. "Good try, Mom. You just let Franklin and Silas keep you safe until we can figure out if the two murders are connected."

"Murders?" Angel's ears perked up. "Like in the movies?"

Granny frowned at Thor. "I'm sorry, Angel; I meant *murders* such as in a flock of crows. A flock of crows is called a *murder* and there are some mean crows in Fuchsia that we are trying to eliminate so they don't hurt anyone."

"Yes, I guess crows aren't like Radish. I was in the yard once and they took my shiny ring that I got out of the candy machine right out of my hand. Did they try and take something from Justine too? Are Silas and Grandpa protecting you so the crows don't get you because you wear shiny things some time?"

"Yes, exactly; you're very smart for your age. Time for everyone to go now and you and for baby Herman to go to sleep." Thor lifted his new son back into his arms.

Franklin ushered Granny and Amelia out of the room. "I'll drop you off, Hermiony, and then take Amelia home."

"Uh, um, I think I'd like to stay at Hermiony's tonight," Amelia said, poking Granny in the arm.

"You would? You want to stay at my house?" Granny questioned.

Amelia poked her again so Franklin couldn't see. "Yes, remember, we have a lot of time to make up for, and I think it would be good if we spent more time together. I just want to bond again with my sister."

Granny reached over and grabbed Amelia before they got into Franklin's car and hugged her tightly to her side in an over-the-top gesture so that Franklin would see. "Yup, bonding time, that's what we need."

Franklin muttered as he got into the car. "Fine, but remember Silas will be right across the street in case there's any trouble."

"Yes, and George and Mavis too," Granny reminded him.

"Double trouble," Franklin stated. "Maybe I should stay, but then again, I repeat, Silas is right across the street."

"That's what I'm counting on," Amelia commented.

Granny gave Amelia a disbelieving look as the Escalade pulled away from the curb.

"Franklin, why haven't you been driving your black, '57 Chevy convertible?" Franklin owned a car just like Granny's but in black.

"It's in my garage, but it only holds two people. I'm thinking of selling it."

"You love that car. It was what brought us together," Granny said, not believing what she was hearing.

"But it's not practical anymore, Hermiony. I'm getting older and with my daughter moving here this fall and now that we have our grandchildren; I decided to get something more conservative."

Amelia's eyes got wide when she saw Granny roll her eyes. She knew what her twin was thinking.

"Fuddy-duddy," Granny muttered.

"What did you say?" Franklin didn't hear the muttered words.

Amelia held her breath waiting for Granny's reply.

"We're here." Granny opened the car door the minute Franklin pulled up in front of the house, saving her from elaborating. Franklin might not have wanted to hear what she wanted to say.

Amelia followed Granny out of the car. Turning to Franklin, Amelia put her hand on his arm through the open window. Granny raised her eyebrows at the gesture.

Franklin patted Amelia's hand and said, "Get a good night's sleep, and remember Silas is right across the street."

He addressed Granny, "Goodnight, Hermiony, when we get this mess straightened out, we need to plan our wedding again. It's coming up soon."

"You have a date set?" Amelia asked in surprise.

"Yes, August 6," Granny answered. She leaned over and gave Franklin a quick kiss through the window.

Franklin beamed at the uncharacteristic gesture. "I'll watch as you two go into the house. It looks like the shysters and the cohorts are still here."

Granny and Amelia turned around to see all the animals perched at Granny's big front window watching them.

"Come on, Amelia, I'll teach you what to feed this crew. They like to eat healthy." Her tone changed to a whisper as they walked to the house, "You and I, we'll have wine and chocolates."

CHAPTER THIRTY

Pounding and crashing woke Granny from a deep sleep. The noise sat her straight up in bed, forcing her to hit the floor with her feet without steadying herself on her bedpost. Trying to get her balance, she weaved down the hallway to the kitchen. The noise had surprised her so much that she hadn't checked to see what she wore to bed the night before.

Amelia rushed into the kitchen at the same time as Granny after having spent the night in an upstairs bedroom. They both stopped when they saw a gaping hole in the side of Granny's kitchen. A face appeared though the hole.

"Starting your new edition today, Granny!" Woodly Spackle grinned through the hole.

"You didn't think to tell me?"

"I did tell you."

Granny frowned. "When?"

"Well, I told your sister when I called your house last night."

Granny looked at Amelia. "You didn't think to tell me? When did he call? I thought we were together until we went to bed."

Amelia shrugged her shoulders. "We were. He didn't talk to me."

Granny turned back to the face in the hole. "What time did you talk to me? Did you call my cell phone?" She turned to Amelia before Woodly had a chance to answer. "Maybe I forgot he called and maybe I forgot I was me and I pretended to be you."

Amelia rolled her eyes at her sister. "That is so you, Hermiony, always trying to blame it on your memory."

Amelia turned to the hole in the wall, "Again, what time did you call and did you call Granny's cell phone and why do you think you talked to her sister?"

"It was about ten—sorry about it being so late—but we'd just finished a job and I wasn't sure till then that we could get here today. So, I called your home phone and the person who answered said she was your sister, although at first I thought it was a man because it had a deeper voice than a woman. Anyway, she said I could call her Gram. I told her I'd be here first thing this morning and she said she'd pass the message along. Sorry, the chat is nice but I have work to do!" With that, he began pounding again.

Granny and Amelia made their way to the living room, deep in thought.

"Franklin said she was dead," Granny murmured.

"She must have been here," Amelia looked around the room.

"Or someone is pretending to be Gram and they're out to make everyone think I'm losing my marbles," Granny suggested.

"You lost your marbles a long time ago," Amelia chuckled. "That was the one game you could never win with Briony."

Granny gave Amelia a long look. "Why are you here? Why did you want to stay the night?"

"I have a plan."

"You have a plan? This ought to be good. I'm sorry, Amelia, but don't you remember? Your plans never worked."

"You had to bring that up, didn't you?"

"Well, if the shoe fits—" Granny smugly reminded her.

"Fine. This plan will work, but we need Silas."

"Why in the world would we trust Silas with our plan? He'd tell Franklin and Thor. And they'd try and stop us."

"But he's not above being a little underhanded."

Granny choked at the word *underhanded,* "And you aren't?"

"Well I can be, I will be, if that's the only way I'm going to find my son."

"We're talking in circles. You haven't told me what this plan that's not going to work is?"

"Get dressed." Amelia looked at what Granny was wearing, "You really wear boring night clothes, Hermiony. If you're going to marry Franklin you'd better get something with a little more pizzazz. I know of a great boutique called Red Hot Momma's over in Brilliant."

Granny looked down at her Granny pj's that she'd put on last night since Amelia was staying. With a sly grin on her face, she answered her sister, "Perhaps I should take your advice, Amelia. Really? A store named Red Hot Momma's? Who knew?"

Granny decided to put on the old outfit that she wore when she worked undercover for the Fuchsia merchants. She dug into her closet and found her old-fashioned flower dress, this time she chose the blue one instead of the red one—it was more understated. She put on her Granny hose and pulled the hose down so it was wrinkly, and finished her ensemble by plopping her hat on top of her head. She then added her red sparkly high-top tennis shoes.

"What happened to you?" Amelia's shocked voice penetrated the air when she saw how Granny had dressed.

"This is my usual garb; I've been on a quest to find myself but I've decided this is who I am."

Amelia was skeptical but decided to save her questions for another time. "Let's go."

"I'm game; where we going?" Granny grabbed her pink pitchfork.

"To see Silas and tell him our plan."

Granny reminded Amelia, "We don't have a plan, you do, and you'd better warn Mr. Supercilious that your plans never work out."

Amelia smiled. "This one will." She held the door open for Granny.

Granny noticed the construction as she stepped onto her porch. Bending down, she picked up a key that was lying on the porch steps. Examining the key, she asked Amelia, "Is this yours?"

Amelia looked at the key that Granny was holding in her hands. "That looks like the key to the factory, but I think I have mine on my keychain." Digging the keychain out of her pocket, she showed Granny the key.

"It does look like the same key. How did it get here?"

"That's a good question; Lars is the only other one who has a key to the factory. Let's go over to the factory after we get done with Silas and find out if this is his key and how it ended up on your porch."

A noise from across the street caught the women's attention. The shysters and the cohorts, along with Radish, who was sitting on Mrs. Bleaty's head, were lined up on the curb watching the construction across the street at Granny's.

Amelia laughed, proceeding across the street to Silas's house, passing the animals on her way. Granny, following Amelia, stopped to address her animals, "Glad you approve! You'll have your own house soon. Then you can stay home instead of visiting Mr. Supercilious. Even you, Radish, I'll adopt you so you don't have to put up with that cantankerous old man."

Silas, answering the door to Amelia's knock, yelled in response, "It's a kennel!"

The shysters and the cohorts, hearing the word *kennel*, began barking and meowing. Mrs. Bleaty bleated and Radish quickly flew through the open door into Silas's house. The rest of the crew ran across the street and into Granny's house through their respective pet doors.

Granny shook her head and moved to join Amelia and Silas. "Apparently, you need to let us in, Silas, Amelia's got a plan and she thinks she needs you. Can't imagine why she'd need a crabby, know-it-all old man. I should warn you, her plans never work out."

Silas led the women into his house. Turning to Amelia, he said, "Always a pleasure, Amelia. What can I help you with?"

Amelia, with tears in her eyes, said, "Oh, Silas, I just have to find my son. Can you help me?" She launched herself into Silas's arms and wept delicately on his shoulder.

Granny watched silently, a suspicious look on her face.

Silas gave Amelia a small hug and patted her back, then held her away from him and gently said, "What's your plan, Amelia? Of course, I'll help."

Granny rolled her eyes, but still stayed silent waiting to hear Amelia's plan.

Amelia sniffed. "If Robert was looking here for our son, then he must have adopted him in this county. I called yesterday to see if I could see the records from that year, but they said adoption records were sealed and locked away. This is a crazy county. They don't do things like the rest of the world. Anyway," Amelia sniffed again and wiped her nose with a tissue that Silas handed to her. "Get this, the records are kept in the judge's chambers. Who does that? I talked to the judge and he won't give me the information I need."

Granny frowned. "So what is your idea? We could hide in the courthouse when it closes and then sneak in and see if we can find something."

Amelia gasped. "Oh, no! That would be illegal. We might get arrested."

Granny shook her head and looked at Silas, "I warn you, her plans never work."

Amelia put her head down on Silas's shoulder. "I need to find my son." She accompanied the words with a few sobs.

Silas again patted her shoulder and then grabbed her shoulders gently and moved her away to look her straight in the face. "Okay, what's your plan?"

Granny again rolled her eyes.

"The county seat is in Ramshackle, fifty miles away. That's where I checked and talked to the judge. I have a friend who makes fake documents—don't ask."

"You have a friend who makes fake documents?" Granny exclaimed. "Amelia, you do amaze me sometime."

Ignoring Granny's outburst, Amelia continued, "We have a fake marriage certificate made up for you two. The judge performs marriages in the room just outside his chambers. You two—Granny and Silas—get married—pretend of course. It won't be legal because of the fake marriage license. The judge's clerks and I will be the witnesses. You only need two witnesses, but we'll say that you think it's good luck to have three. While the marriage is being performed, I'll pretend to not feel well and slip away to the bathroom in the judge's chambers. Take a little while saying your vows. Anyway, I'll see if I can find the old adoption records. We'll leave and no one will be the wiser." Amelia flashed a big grin at Granny and Silas. "After all, who would suspect subterfuge by two old women and an old man?"

"Subterfuge." Granny shook her head, "That's the most scatterbrained idea I've ever heard of and it's going to end up with us in the hoosegow."

Silas cackled, "When has that ever bothered you before? Getting soft in your old age, Mrs. Persnickulous?"

"I warn you this isn't going to work. When are we doing this?" asked Granny.

"I have it set for Monday morning. We can't tell anyone, especially Franklin," Amelia instructed.

"I happen to know he's going to be busy on Monday," Silas informed the women. "Thor's taking the week off because of little Herman so Franklin's going to be working with Ephraim. They still don't have any idea why Justine was murdered. Franklin's going out of town to question Justine's family. He's asked me to watch out for you two, and I guess that's what I'll be doing on Monday. Count me in."

"Remember I warned you. It's going to be an orange jumpsuit for all of us or else the wrinkle farm for all of us when my kids find this out. It's strange that Penelope and Starshine haven't been nosing around my life," Granny commented.

"We have to go," Amelia announced.

"Go where?" Silas asked, suspicious of Amelia's announcement.

Granny answered Silas's query, "To the chocolate factory."

"Um, yes, um, Granny hasn't tasted our chocolate."

"I'll drive you," said Silas.

"Nope, no chocolate for you," Granny informed him.

"Maybe we should tell him about the phone call," Amelia said in a soft voice.

"Phone call?" asked Silas.

Granny gave Amelia a stern look. "Oh….the phone call….yes. The florist has time open for us today to pick out the flowers for my wedding. It's going to be a full day. See you later, Silas." Granny grabbed Amelia's arm and hustled her out of Silas's house.

"Amelia, Silas is on a need to know basis and believe me when I tell you he doesn't need to know. Got that? I have so much to teach you."

CHAPTER THIRTY-ONE

The police gave permission for Amelia's chocolate factory to continue on with their preparations for their opening in October. Granny and Amelia found Lars in the office chatting with the designer, Crunch Drizzle, about the demo kitchen where visitors would be able to take instructions in creating chocolate candies at home. The chocolate store, which would be located on the premises, would be right next to the demo kitchen. Crunch also was a chocolatier and would be working with them in creating their chocolates.

"Crunch, good to see you," Amelia greeted her friend.

Crunch looked back and forth from Amelia to Granny. "I'm seeing double!"

Amelia laughed as Granny stepped forward and eyed the chocolatier. "Granny here, I'm a dear; chocolates' my second name, I like your game."

Crunch laughed. "The pleasure's all mine. Since you like chocolate so much and it's obvious you're related to Amelia, perhaps you could be our new chocolate taster."

Granny's eyes lit up at the offer.

Lars spoke up, "We could make that happen, Aunt Hermiony. I am your nephew."

"I've got to be going. Time to for this Crunch to crunch some chocolate numbers," Crunch chuckled, walking out of the room laughing at his own play on words.

"Lars, do you have the key to the factory?" Amelia questioned.

"Right here on my key ring, why?"

Granny stepped forward. "Because we found a key that looks like it belongs to the factory door on my front step.

Amelia showed him the key. Frowning, Lars took the key out of Amelia's hands and left the room. He came back a few minutes later.

"It's the factory key, all right."

"Lars, I….oh, someone's here?"

Ella Delure, Delight's daughter, entered the room.

"Ella, what are you doing here?" Granny gave Lars a suspicious look.

"Ah, hi, Granny, I ah…was applying for a job." Ella glanced at Lars.

"Yes, yes, I'll get you that application." Lars took Ella's arm and led her from the room.

Granny wrinkled her nose. "If you believe that, I've got some trees I can sell you in Latvia."

"I believe that's land in China," Amelia countered.

Lars came back into the room.

"Now about the key," Granny reminded him.

"We do have an extra key," he said.

"We do?" Amelia questioned. "I didn't give permission to give out extra keys."

Lars looked uncomfortable. "I gave a key to ah..ah…Starshine. That's probably why you found it on your steps."

"I love my niece, but why does she need a key?"

"Yes," Granny echoed Amelia's sentiments, "Why does my daughter need a key to the chocolate factory. It doesn't quite fit with her hippy image. By the way, what happened to your hippie image? You seem quite the polished fellow now.

"Oh, he was testing the waters when he met Starshine and fell in love, now he has to polish his image a little so he can fit in with the factory. Although, I do think you're a little too polished, Lars. This is Fuchsia and Fuchsia allows each person to be their own unique self and that suit doesn't quite look like you or Fuchsia," Amelia observed.

"We're off the subject which is the key," said Granny. "I'll ask Starshine if she's the one who answered the phone at my house last night since we found the key at my house."

Lars jumped at Granny's words. "No, no! Don't do that! Let me handle it. Starshine doesn't want you to know she was at your house. It's supposed to be a surprise."

Granny and Amelia stared at Lars for a moment before Granny said, "I don't like surprises so you'd better tell Starshine and her conspirators. Got that!" Granny took her pitchfork and poked Lars in the chest with the handle.

Amelia stepped between Granny and Lars. "He's a good boy, Hermiony, and he's my boy and he's your nephew. Cut him a little slack. Apparently, he's in cahoots with your daughters. Maybe that's why they've been so silent lately."

Granny put down her pitchfork.

Lars heaved a sigh of relief.

"Drop me off at my house, Hermiony, I need a day of rest. I'm sure Franklin's looking for us." Just then, Amelia nodded in the direction of the door. "Speak of the devil."

Amelia quickly turned and opened the doors on a cabinet in the corner. Pulling a couple of boxes out, she handed them to Granny. "Franklin, Silas! How nice! I was just giving Granny some samples of our chocolates. I brought her here for a tour of the factory."

Granny nodded. "Yup, Amelia, nice factory but I still think you should put in the roller-coaster chocolate ride. That's a good idea to drop chocolates in the customers' mouths when they come around the last curve."

Lars shook his head in confusion. Amelia, seeing Lars was about to open his mouth, stuffed a piece of chocolate in it. "What do you think Lars? Is this kind too creamy?" Smiling sweetly, she took Silas's arm and led him out of the office. Granny stuffed a second piece in Lars's mouth as she took Franklin's arm and led him out the door. "You know what they say; life is like pieces of chocolate in your mouth."

CHAPTER THIRTY-TWO

There was no pounding when Granny woke up on Sunday morning. Woodly Spackle had put a temporary barrier up in the kitchen where the hole was, and where French doors would lead to the new shyster and cohort apartments. Granny pushed the button to brew her coffee and checked the pet dishes to make sure the animals had eaten their food before they left the previous night on their nighttime journeys. Mr. Pigster still wasn't too sure about wandering around town so he stayed at Granny's house most days, missing out on Granny's rescue and the curb sitting to watch the new rooms go up. This morning, Granny had left him snuggled underneath her bed.

Taking out her favorite coffee cup that said, "You're better off dead than wed," Granny sat down to enjoy the peace and quiet of her house. She closed her eyes and tried to picture Robert Blackford. Who had he hung out with while he lived in Fuchsia? She couldn't remember. They'd never spent any time with friends. Life together was so exciting that they didn't need friends, at least, that's what he said. Why would he come back here all these years later to look for his son if he didn't have friends or family here? And why would his brother have been helping him? Why would he come here after breaking out of jail?

Granny shook her head. There seemed to be too many lose ends. Poor Justine, finding her father and then being murdered, why? Was Jack Puffleman telling the truth?

Granny picked up her cell phone to call Starshine to see if she was the one answering the phone the night Woodly called. Granny put the phone down. She didn't want to ruin the surprise for Starshine and Penelope.

Her phone rang. "Granny here. No, I don't drink beer."

"Hermiony, I'll pick you up for church in a half hour."

"Franklin, I guess it would be nice to see a little bit of you. What about Amelia?"

"Amelia is going to church with Lars. She'll be fine."

"Franklin, when are you going to tell us why you're watching us like hawks? Wouldn't it better if we knew who's supposed to be after us?"

"Thirty minutes." Franklin hung up without answering Granny's questions.

Finishing her coffee, Granny trekked back to her bedroom to get dressed. She could hear Mr. Pigster snoring away. She hoped the pig would soon feel more comfortable when the new apartments were finished. Again, Granny decided to don her Granny clothes for church.

She was ready when Franklin beeped the horn indicating he was there. Locking the door, she eyed her pink pitchfork that she'd left on the porch last night. She'd leave it home. After all, what could happen at church again that she would need it? She thought about her wedding that didn't happen.

It was a comfortable drive to We Save You Christian Church. Franklin and Granny stuck to safe subjects. They talked about nothing—meaning the weather, flowers and other generic subjects. Granny knew there was more of something just sitting under the surface that needed to be said but she left it alone for another day.

Pastor Henrietta was again the preacher for the day. She explained why she'd been preaching so many Sundays in a row. "Youth trip, Fishing trip, camp trip, Catholic Priest tripped!"

Granny saw that Tricky Travis Trawler was again in the pew waiting to pilfer from the collection plate. She indicated to Franklin that she was going to sit next to Tricky. Franklin followed her to the pew. Soon Amelia and Lars joined them on the other side of Tricky. Amelia was dressed almost identically to Granny this morning except her dress was green. Granny smiled when she saw Tricky look first at her and then at Amelia. Amelia winked at Granny.

Pastor Henrietta gave a nice sermon on little white lies. At the end, she made an announcement, "I'm so happy to announce that Franklin Jester Gatsby and Hermiony Vidalia Criony Fiddlestadt have again set a wedding date and will be married in this church on August 6th. The bride and groom will not be sending out invitations but everyone is invited to attend."

At the announcement, Granny sat up straight and whispered to Franklin, "You invited everyone?"

Franklin nodded. "I want everyone to experience our joy."

"You didn't consult me?" Granny's voice was still a whisper.

"Didn't see the need; thought you'd be happy about it."

Granny stood up, moved past Franklin and out of the pew. "Well, let me tell you something Franklin Jester Gatsby," the entire congregation turned when they heard Granny's loud voice, "apparently you still thought I was on a need to know basis and I didn't need to know. Well…….here's something you need to know, when I'm not on a need to know basis, then you're on a need to know basis and I'm not telling you what you need to know. Figure it out for yourself!" Granny turned and walked out of church leaving Franklin open-mouthed.

Pastor Henrietta, still on the podium, inquired of Franklin, "I didn't quite understand that, did you Franklin?"

Amelia reached across Tricky Travis and patted Franklin's arm. "I'll decipher, Pastor Henrietta," Amelia said, standing up. "The wedding's off!" Amelia sat back down.

CHAPTER THIRTY-THREE

"Make sure you dress like a bride," Amelia instructed.

Granny barked into the phone, "The pretend bride, you mean. I wasn't born in a barnyard."

"Silas will pick you up and then he'll pick me up and we'll go to Ramshackle. The pretend wedding is set for 11:00 a.m. I have the fake marriage license."

"What time will my persnickety groom be picking me up?" Granny asked.

"At 9:30 a.m., which will give us time to prepare and plan. Wear red; it'll prove you're not dead."

Amelia hung up, leaving no one to hear Granny mutter, "You can't rhyme and this plan isn't fine."

Mr. Pigster snuffled at Granny's feet as she pulled the red dress out of her closet that Mavis had her buy during her makeover."

"Do you like this, Mr. Pigster? It better work."

Shuffling to the bathroom in her flip flops, she looked in the mirror to check out her hair. She'd decided that for her mock wedding she would wear it down. Possibly no one would recognize her with her hair down and wearing her fancy red dress. She'd even put on red heels to match the dress. Though Ramshackle was fifty miles away, it was chancy that she might run in to someone she knew. It would be better to go incognito.

Going back to her closet, she rummaged around until she found the hat she was looking for. It was a pill box type but it had a veil that came down over the front to shadow her face. She was a pretend bride, after all, and didn't brides still wear veils?

Mr. Pigster snorted and ran back under the bed. "Hmm, must be a good disguise if he doesn't recognize me," Granny said to the empty house.

She heard a beep outside the door. Silas was there. She was going to take her pitchfork for the occasion, just in case they got caught and they had to make a fast getaway she could pin the judge to the wall while the others got out.

She was almost to Silas's car when Mavis *hoo haa*'d from across the street, "Where ya going? Did I miss an invitation to a costume party?"

Granny acknowledged Mavis, "No, just practice for a new reality show starting up in Fuchsia."

Mavis perked up. "A new reality show? Where? Can I come along?"

"I'll get you the information. I have to go."

She was about to open the car door when Penelope came running across the street yelling, "Mom, why are you dressed like that? I haven't seen that dress since the wedding. I can't remember."

Granny peered into the car at Silas. He grinned and shook his head. He wasn't going to get her out of this one. "I'm going to have my picture taken for a Christmas present for my family. Something for you to remember me by, but—shh—it's a secret. Don't tell you brother or your sister. I want it to be a surprise."

"Oh, Mom, that's a wonderful idea! I love that. Maybe we can have a family picture in August when you and Franklin get married."

Granny nodded her head. "Yes, I'll keep that in mind. We have to go. Franklin's out of town, so Silas is driving me. I don't want to be late."

Granny slid into the car and shut the door and instructed Silas, "Hit it before someone else sees us."

Silas pulled away from the curb as Granny sweetly smiled and waved at Penelope.

Silas looked Granny up and down and said, "You clean up good, woman."

Granny took a look at Silas in his suit and said, "Ditto to you."

Amelia was waiting for them on the sidewalk in front of her house. She slid into the back seat. "Speed up, Silas; we're going to be late. What took you so long?"

"A reality show and family pictures," Granny quipped.

"Huh?"

"Never mind, Amelia; tell us the plan for today. You should be used to Granny's speech," Silas reminded Amelia.

"The ceremony is at 11:00 a.m.," said Amelia. "It will take place right outside the judge's chambers. The story is that you want to get married there rather than Fuchsia because you want a simple wedding without all the drama of your children who are worried that they'll lose their inheritance if you get married."

"Their inheritance?" Granny guffawed, "Yah, right, they'll lose the shysters and the cohorts. I left them to my children."

"Anyway," Amelia continued, "You'll sign the marriage license, of course; it's not legal, but the judge doesn't know that."

"I don't want to burst your bubble, Amelia, but what happens when the judge finds out?" Granny asked.

"We'll cross that bridge when we come to it," she replied.

Silas shook his head. "How about we stop crossing bridges and bursting bubbles and cut to the chase."

"Fine." Amelia got a stubborn look on her face and said, "This is going to work, but if you're both chicken then you can drop out and I'll find someone else I can pay to help me do this."

"She's your sister after all, Hermiony," Silas chuckled.

"Of course, she learned from the best," said Granny, "go on, Amelia."

The ceremony will start and I'll pretend to be a little woozy and break into the ceremony. I'll tell the judge to go on and I'll get back in time for the *I do's*. I'll ask if I can use the restroom in his office and get a drink. The ceremony will continue and I'll hunt for the adoption records from that year. My sources tell me that they're not locked up. This county court office lives in the back ages and still won't open adoption records. Apparently, no one has challenged them and I don't have time for that."

They arrived at the courthouse. Amelia insisted that she and Granny go into the ladies room to poof up Granny's hair and put on some make up. Granny didn't usually wear too much make up and hadn't' thought to put any on that morning, but Amelia came prepared and gussied Granny up.

"Enough, Amelia, it's not like this is real wedding."

"We want the judge to think it is. Now, let's practice the *you're-in-love* smile."

"The *what*!" Granny yelped.

"You have to look like you're in love. Now, pretend I'm Franklin and look at me."

Granny screwed up her face with a smile.

"No, Hermiony, you're not in pain."

"For Pete's sake, Amelia, no one cares. You should have just told them we have to get married and that I'm pregnant." Granny hooted at the thought.

"You need to take this seriously. My son hinges on it."

Granny patted Amelia's cheek. "Okay, okay, I get it; let's go."

Silas was waiting for them outside the ladies' room. He looked keenly at Granny's face. "Something different, I can't quite put my finger on it. You're flushed; are you feeling okay?"

Granny tapped Silas in the chest. "You old coot, that's blush. Can't you tell? It's fake but you probably haven't had anyone blush at you in so long, you don't recognize it."

"Enough, you two!" Amelia whispered, "You're supposed to be in love. Let's go to the judge's chambers."

The judge's assistant met them in the front office, "The judge will be with you in a minute."

Amelia made the introductions, "This is Hermiony Fiddlestadt and Silas Crickett. I'm Amelia, Hermiony's sister. So nice of the judge to take this wedding on such short notice."

The assistant nodded. "When he heard your story, Amelia, he understood. He loves a love story."

"And they love each other so much, don't you, Silas and Hermiony?" Amelia beamed at the couple and poked Hermiony in the ribs.

"Yes, yes, we do," Granny said, putting on her best fake smile. "Silas is the love of my life; you could say he is the poke to my needle, the edge to my knife."

Granny was about to continue when Amelia broke in, "Yes, yes! We get it." Amelia smiled at Silas.

Silas grabbed Granny and hugged her close. "She's the crick in my neck, the pepper to my salt."

Granny moved her elbow back into Silas's stomach. Silas let her go with a laugh.

Amelia was relieved when Judge Olaria walked in.

Judge Olaria shook Silas's and Granny's hands. He had the marriage license in his hand. "This was put on my desk this morning. All you two have to do is sign it, here and here. He handed the pen to Granny.

Granny hesitated. Amelia poked her and whispered in her ear, "It doesn't mean anything; it's fake. Take a good look at it."

Granny hadn't seen a marriage license since she married Ferdinand, so it looked fine to her. She signed her name and handed the pen to Silas. Silas signed his name under Granny's.

"Fine, now shall we begin. I need to call my other assistant from my office. He went back into the office and came out with another young woman. "This is Kelly. She's the other witness. I was surprised when your sister said you needed three."

Amelia spoke up, "What I didn't tell you is that I have a condition and there are times I need to leave the room abruptly so I knew I couldn't be counted on to be here for the entire ceremony. Sometimes this condition comes on just like this," Amelia snapped her fingers. "And I wanted them to be able to finish the ceremony."

Judge Olaria nodded. "I understand. If you need it, my office is open. Feel free to use the restroom, lay down on the couch or get some water if you want."

Amelia nodded. "Thank you, but please finish the ceremony even if I have to leave for a few minutes. Those *I do's* are so important."

Granny coughed to cover the laughter bubbling up inside of her. She didn't know Amelia had it in her.

The office assistant stuck a bouquet of flowers in Granny's hands and put a rose on Silas's lapel. Silas was silent, not believing what he heard coming from the sisters.

Judge Olaria flicked a switch and music played in the background. The strains of *Lover's Concerto* by the Toys accompanied the judge's words.

Granny turned and whispered to Amelia who was still next to her, "You chose *Lover's Concerto* as our fake wedding music? Couldn't you have chosen *These Boots Are Made For Walkin'* by Nancy Sinatra?"

Silas poked Granny to make her pay attention. He whispered to Hermiony as the Judge spoke the first words of the wedding ceremony. "Quiet, she's got to get away; you're messing with her plan."

Granny adoringly looked into Silas's eyes. "Silas, dear, the plan isn't going to work." She turned to listen to the judge.

"Friends, we have been invited here today to share with Hermiony and Silas a very important moment in their lives. In the year they have known each other, their love and understanding of each other has grown and matured, and now they have decided to live their lives together as husband and wife. Who supports this couple in their marriage?"

Amelia stepped forward. "I do." Amelia swayed sideways and caught the arm of the judge, batted her eyes at him and said, "Oh my, I need to leave for a few minutes; please go on."

The judge patted Amelia's hand, "Go ahead, my dear. I'm so sorry this happened, but I'll take care of them and you can hear the ceremony from my office. Are you sure you don't want me to stop?"

Amelia again batted her eyes at the judge, "No, I don't have long and it's so important that I see them married. Please continue." She turned and made her way through the door of the judge's chambers.

The judge cleared his throat. "Shall we continue?"

Silas looked at Hermiony with a twinkle in his eye, "Yes, please." Silas took both of Hermiony's hands in his.

"This is a reading I wrote myself." The judge shuffled his papers. "Today we are gathered here to witness something spectacular. Two people who have survived the hardships of life, two people who in the face of adversity and strife in their family, with their relationship, against all odds are going to risk sharing a life together. They say love conquers all, and these two people are not afraid to go forward risking the wrath of those they love to be together in the final years of their lives. They will grow old together, grow sick together, and finally forever after, go to the big cloud in the sky, knowing they did it their way. Hermiony and Silas went up the water spout, down came the rain and washed the doubts all out, out came the sun and dried up all the rain and Silas and Hermiony were never the same again.

Silas mouthed to Hermiony, "Wacko words."

Hermiony nodded in agreement.

The judge continued as Hermiony looked out of the side of her eye for Amelia. She was still in the judge's chambers. The two office assistants seemed entranced with the wedding and hardly took their eyes off the judge.

"Hermiony and Silas, the institution of marriage is a very serious one. You are creating a life together, to share, to be honest, to not hold back any secrets. You will become one in spirit. When others may try to part you, you must chain yourselves together to the pier to stay strong and steady so the pirates can't steal your treasure. Take it seriously, eat ice cream before you go to bed and always drink coffee in the morning to wake you up so you can deal with your spouse's wrinkles."

Silas squeezed Hermiony's hands tighter so she couldn't get them loose to assault the judge. She opened her mouth to respond to the judge's words, when Silas pulled her forward and kissed her, whispering against her lips, "You're gonna blow it. Remember Vitale."

The judge cleared his throat, "It's not time for the kiss yet. Now shall we proceed?"

Silas let go of Granny and they both stepped back to listen to the judge.

The music in the background changed to *Lighting Strikes* by Lou Christie.

Granny whispered to Silas, "I'm going to get back at Amelia for these songs."

"Proceed," Silas answered the judge.

Let us begin. Silas, did you write your own vows?"

"Vows?" Silas's bewildered expression conveyed his answer. "Did you?" he asked Hermiony.

"No, but we can wing it. At least, I can, Mr. Supercilious."

"Fine, we'll wing it." Turning to the judge, he said, "I'm ready." Silas turned back to Hermiony. "Hermiony, the first time I saw you, I knew you were trouble. Then you took me on a ride and nearly killed me. Added to that, you put my son in prison and you can't cook. All the things I never looked for in a bride. I give you this ring with no conditions. I accept your colorful personality, your willful ways and your sparkling independence along with your crabbiness."

The Granny spoke, "First, I want to say, Silas, I've heard those last words before. You stole Franklin's lines. Silas, you are the most ornery coot I know. You're always interrupting my plans, you bring me creepy creatures, and you don't know the meaning of the words *it's on a need to know basis.* You team up with my fiancé," Granny realized what she'd said and looked at the judge, but he seemed not to have heard, so she continued on, "to watch me all the time. You're a stalker. I'll give you a ring for your finger and not your neck, although I want to wring it most of the time."

"Do you have the rings?" the judge asked.

Both Hermiony and Silas shook their heads.

The office assistant Kelly chimed in, "I do. Amelia gave them to me before she had to retire to the office."

"We have rings?" Hermiony whispered to Silas. "Are you sure this isn't real?"

As the judge continued, Hermiony looked around to see if Amelia was back—she wasn't.

"Do you Silas Crickett, take Hermiony Vidalia Criony Fiddlestadt, to be your wife?"

"I do." Silas slipped the ring on Hermiony's finger.

"Do you Hermiony Vidalia Criony Fiddlestadt, take Silas Crickett to be your husband?"

"I do."

"Then by the power invested in me, I pronounce you man and wife. You may kiss the bride."

Silas turned Hermiony toward him and kissed her just as Amelia arrived back in the room. "Oh no! I missed it. I'm so sorry." Amelia hugged Hermiony, tugging her away from Silas. Amelia whispered into Granny's ear, "I have something; let's get out of here."

"It's time to go," Granny's abrupt manner told Silas not to argue.

"Bye Judge Olaria," Amelia waved. "Thanks for everything."

With a twinkle in his eye, the judge winked at Amelia, "You bet!"

CHAPTER THIRTY-FOUR

"I got it. I got it!" Amelia's gleeful cry could be heard down the street.

"Well, we'll get it if someone realizes what we've done. You shouldn't have used our real names, Amelia," Granny chided.

"Let's head back to Fuchsia and see what you've got." Silas took off towards his car."

"Is that any way to treat your bride?" Amelia chastised him when they reached the car.

"Can it, Amelia. The charades are over; where's the papers?" Granny watched as Amelia pulled them out of her small bosom."

"Get in the car. We can talk about this on the way back to Fuchsia," Silas ordered.

Amelia looked back. "It doesn't seem as if anyone has caught on yet, nobody appears to be looking for us." Amelia's sly smile was caught by Granny.

"What are you smiling about?"

Amelia shook her head. "Well, my plan worked. There was only one adoption that year, so it wasn't too hard to find once I picked the lock on the file. Apparently, the judge does lock his papers up."

Granny shook her head. "It appears that way. You've grown over the years, Amelia."

"What does it say?" Silas asked, keeping his eyes on the road.

The paper, folded in tiny squares, still sat in her lap. Amelia was staring at the paper but not attempting to open it.

Granny grabbed the paper off Amelia's lap, unfolded it and began to read, "Male baby adopted to Carissa and Douglas Melborne of Brilliant, Minnesota."

"Never heard the name before." Amelia shook her head."

"Me neither, but I didn't mingle much out on the farm with Ferdinand. Maybe Delight or Lulu would know the name. They've lived here all their lives and they shop in Brilliant," Granny suggested.

"What about Ditty Belle and her Fuchsia book? Does she have a history of Brilliant?" Amelia suggested.

Granny tapped Silas on the shoulder. "Mr. Supercilious, drop us off at the Pink Percolator so we can talk to Delight."

"Don't you think we should tell Thor?" Amelia suggested. "Maybe he could find out."

Granny shook her head. "No, he's busy with his new baby Herman, and the Tall Guy and the Fuchsia police are all busy with the murders. We can handle this."

Silas shook his head. "I'll drop you at the Pink Percolator on one condition—that you stay there until Franklin or I pick you up. I'm going to find old Snowshoe and send him over to Brilliant to do some snooping and see if he can find this family. Got that!"

"Why, Silas, of course we'll stay there. A bride must wait for her groom," Granny's innocent voice didn't fool Silas.

"Woman, you're in danger, you almost got run down once," Silas reminded her.

"From who?" Granny yelled. "Tell me from who and I'll know who to look out for! I think you just told me Gram Gramstead was dead to throw me off the scent. You're just like Franklin, always trying to control what I do."

Realizing what she'd just said, Granny became silent. By her words, she realized that she'd just admitted that Franklin had some of the same traits as her late husband Ferdinand.

Amelia cleared her throat. "We're here. Silas, we'll be fine. Find my son." She grabbed Granny's arm and dragged her out of the car.

"Let go of me," Granny rasped, "We're going to find your son and solve the mystery of who I'm supposed to be afraid of. Let the police solve the murder, because there will be another one when I find out who's out to get me." Granny slammed the tines of the pitchfork that she'd quickly grabbed out of Silas's car on the sidewalk before he drove away."

Amelia laughed at the sight of Granny hitting the sidewalk with the tines of the fork. "Careful, Hermiony, you'll bend instead of fork."

Delight was watching through the window and had the door open for the two women, waiting to see what was up.

"What's happening? Why did we cancel our midnight meeting? Wait, we need coffee and sweets." Delight hurried away.

"Maybe we should go out on the donut patio. It appears empty. No one will hear us," Granny suggested.

"Delight, we'll be out here." Amelia pointed to the patio.

Granny and Amelia were quiet as they watched the donut fountain, which today was spouting pink whipped cream.

They heard Delight's giggle before they saw Delight. "Makes you just want to jump in and cover yourself in whipped cream, doesn't it?"

Granny winked at her sister. "Why, Delight, we didn't know you had such risqué thoughts. Do we have a boutique for you!"

Delight blushed as she set the coffee down. "Well, I've been seeing someone. Do you know Silas's friend Humboldt Notorious?"

"Nope, never heard of him," Granny continued, "Delight, have you ever heard of a family by the name of Carissa and Doug Melborne?"

Delight thought for a moment then said, "No, don't believe I have, why?"

Amelia whispered, "We think they adopted my Vitale."

"Why are you whispering, Amelia?" asked Delight.

Granny shook her head. "She thinks we're still at the courthouse."

Delight's eyes opened wide. "Courthouse? What courthouse? Why were you at the courthouse?"

Granny saw Amelia open her mouth, but before she could answer, Granny interrupted, "To find the records." Granny stood up. "We have to go."

"Where are we going?" Amelia asked.

"We need to have a meal. Delight's coffee and this cream-filled, tree-shaped concoction was delicious, but I need some fried chicken. We'll head to Rack's. Do you ever miss your forest, Delight?" Granny was referring to the trees that were now in her back yard.

"Yes, in fact, I'm thinking of purchasing some land behind the Pink Percolator and reviving Ella's Enchanted Forest."

Granny frowned. "Speaking of Ella, I didn't know she was changing jobs."

"Changing jobs?" Delight's confusion was evident because of the look on her face.

"Why yes," Amelia answered, "She was at my chocolate factory applying for a job, at least that's what Lars said."

Delight giggled. "That Lars of yours is such a sweet boy. I miss him working here. He always made Ella laugh and me too."

Amelia reminded her sister, "Your, uh, I mean, Silas said we should wait here for him."

"We're just going to Rack's; it's only a few blocks away. Delight, tell him to meet us there."

"Why don't we call him?" Amelia suggested nervously.

"We'll be fine," Granny assured her. "Now come on." Granny led the way out of the patio through the back alley.

"Look, Granny, did you forget your car again?" Amelia pointed down the alley.

Granny peered at the '57 Chevy parked at the end of the alley. "Can't be my car, my car's home in the garage."

"Do you want to check it out?"

"Good idea. Amazing! Another plan that might work." Granny led the way, holding tightly to her pink pitchfork.

The top on the car was down. Granny looked around before getting in. "Looks like my car."

"Maybe we should call the Tall Guy or Silas or Franklin?" Amelia was dancing around nervously.

"Well, there's only one way to know for sure." Granny reached in her pocket and got out her keychain. "I really need to start carrying my pocketbook again. These keys weigh down my dress."

Granny took the key and put it into the ignition and turned. The car started right up. "Yup, it's my car. How did it get here?"

Amelia got in the passenger side. "Did you forget you left it here?"

"Amelia, would I forget driving my car downtown?"

"Yes." Amelia's foot touched something under the seat. She reached down and brought out a red wig.

Granny frowned. "Last I saw this red wig it was on Snowshoe Notorious's head. He must have something to do with this. Call Silas and tell him to get ol' Snowshoe down to Racks with him."

"You're going to confront him?"

Granny smiled. "Reach out and pick up my pitchfork that I left on the sidewalk there, Amelia. We might need it."

CHAPTER THIRTY-FIVE

Granny and Amelia were sitting at Granny's favorite booth when Silas and Snowshoe Notorious joined them.

"I thought I told you to wait at the Pink Percolator!" Silas bellowed as he slid into the booth across from Granny.

Humboldt slid in next to Silas.

"Humboldt, nice to see you," Granny said sweetly, right before pulling the red wig she'd been concealing on her lap onto the table. With a flip, she tossed it at Humboldt. "Or should I say Gram Gramstead wannabee?"

Humboldt looked at Silas and then back at Granny with a blank expression, "Who?"

Granny tapped the table so hard the water in her water glass shook. "You've been trying to make me think Gram Gramstead is back and after me! You've been trying to make me think I can't think anymore!"

"What?" Humboldt asked, a look of confusion on his face.

Silas laughed. "It's Granny speak."

"You!" Granny pointed her dinner fork at Silas. "You're probably in on this too!"

"Uh, Hermiony, you shouldn't talk to your husband like that." Amelia touched Granny's arm.

Granny shook Amelia's hand off of her arm. "He's not my husband! That was your scam, so I'll talk to the ornery, scheming coot any way I want! They're trying to send me to the wrinkle farm or to the hoosegow."

Silas shook his head. "Suppose you tell us what this is all about. I saw your car out front. Did you go back home and get it?"

"No! He stole it from my garage and parked it at the corner of the alley by the Pink Percolator!"

"What?" Humboldt turned to Silas. "You warned me about her."

"Humboldt was with me," said Silas. "I filled him in on what we discovered and he's going to head over to Brilliant to see what he can find out about this Carissa and Douglas Melbourne. There's another thing to consider. Humboldt reminded me that Robert Blackford was going by the name Melborne Shultz in Canada. Maybe the *Shultz* is another clue. He must have named himself so he'd remember where his son was. Somehow, he must have known," Silas concluded.

"Afternoon, can I take your order?" Gretchen addressed Silas and Humboldt.

"Give them the same as Amelia and me,." Granny ordered.

"Did you hear?" Gretchen leaned forward whispering, "The police are at AbStract. Word on the street's that it has something to do with Justine's murder. Apparently, Jack Puffleman was her father and now he's a suspect in her murder."

"He didn't do it!" Granny declared.

All eyes turned to Granny.

"You know this how?" Silas questioned.

"I talked to Jack Puffleman," said Granny. "He told me he was Justine's father. We saw him leaving AbStract through the underground street door the night of the murder, so I questioned him."

Silas raised his eyebrows at her words. "And of course you told Thor all this? And what do you mean by *we*? I thought you were all at a slumber party at Amelia's all night."

Amelia, wanting to help her sister, jumped in, "We took a little walk—exercise, you know—in the underground streets, good for the soul. It was just by chance that we saw him. Actually, none of us remember we saw him. Only Granny saw him because we all had our eyes closed while we were walking. It was too light down there for a walk in the dark."

Granny put her hand over Amelia's mouth. "We need to go and see what's happening. Move, Amelia, so I can out!"

As Amelia began to move out of the booth, they saw Franklin walk in the door of the restaurant. Granny grabbed Amelia's arm to pull her back into the booth. Franklin saw them and came back and grabbed a chair so he could sit at the end of the booth.

"Glad I found all of you," he said. "Saw your car, Granny, when I was going to check on Amelia."

"Franklin," said Silas, "this is Humboldt Snowshoe, an old friend and detective from Alaska."

Franklin looked questioningly at Snowshoe. "I thought you were the lawyer Silas hired for Granny when she was almost arrested?"

Humboldt looked uncomfortable. "Well, yes, I do that too in time of need."

"What's the news?" Granny asked Franklin.

"We've arrested Jack Puffleman for Justine's murder," said Franklin. "It turns out that he's Justine's real father and apparently, he didn't want Justine to tell his family. We found his DNA at the crime scene. Justine's murder didn't have anything to do with what happened at your farm, Hermiony. It was a coincidence."

"He didn't do it," Granny declared.

"Hermiony, we know all about your seeing him coming out of the store the night that Justine was murdered. He said you were his alibi. But by all accounts, that was around midnight and Justine was murdered before midnight."

"Why were Justine and her real father at my chocolate factory and how did they get in?" Amelia wondered.

"Well," replied Franklin, "apparently Justine had a key."

"What! That's news to me," said Amelia, standing up in the booth. Granny pulled her back down. "How did she get a key?"

"According to your stepson Lars, it was stolen off the wall in his office," said Franklin.

"But we found the key on Granny's front steps," Amelia informed him.

"You couldn't have. The key was on Justine's body," Franklin countered.

"He didn't do it!" Granny said again.

"Look, Hermiony, we know you have a soft spot for Jack Puffleman because you worked undercover for him, but stress and a big secret such as this about to be revealed makes people do strange things." Franklin reached past Amelia and patted Granny's hand.

Amelia started to cough. She sipped a glass of water. Choking out her words, she said, "You'll have to excuse me." Sliding out of the booth, she slipped out the back door of Racks and could be seen going to her house across the street.

Franklin, concerned, said, "Maybe I should go and see if she's all right."

Granny nodded. "You do that, Franklin. We're not finished here."

Franklin kissed Granny on the cheek and left to find Amelia.

Granny looked at Silas. "You've been awfully quiet. Now Snowshoe or gumshoe or whoever you are, why are you stalking me wearing this red wig?"

Snowshoe Notorious shook his head. "I'm not stalking you, Granny. I found the red wig in Silas's bushes."

Granny's eyes shot daggers at Silas. "You did this or you're lying to me about Gram."

Silas shook his head. "Gram is dead, Granny. You probably just forgot your car. And the red wig? Someone's playing a joke on you. Come on, we'll follow you home. You'd better check on your new addition. It looked like Mrs. Bleaty was trying to help Woodly with the siding. He would put some siding on and Mrs. Bleaty would take it off. Did you consult with her about the color?

CHAPTER THIRTY-SIX

Mavis and George, along with Penelope and Butch, were all at Granny's when she pulled into the driveway. Mavis had Mrs. Bleaty by her collar and was talking to her soothingly. Butch was sitting, leaning back on Baskerville. Penelope was holding Fish and Furball on her lap, and George managed to have one arm around Little White Poodle and the other around Tank. Mr. Pigster was quietly lazing under a tree.

"Why are you all here?" Granny reached down to pet Mr. Pigster.

"I asked them to help," Woodly Spackle yelled down from his ladder.

"The animals were trying to stop him from siding your new addition," Penelope explained. "We were all outside when he hollered for help."

Granny gazed at the siding already on the house. "They must not have liked the color I picked."

Penelope shook her head. "I don't think they care about color, Mom."

Silas came to join the group after parking his car in his driveway. "Remember, they belong to this crotchety old woman. They might be just as finicky too."

"Let them loose and let's ask them," Granny ordered.

Penelope rolled her eyes as she loosened her grip on the two shysters she was holding.

"I got it," Mavis exclaimed. "George, run home and get those color swatches we use for our *Color Is Overwhelming* reality show."

George let loose of his two shysters so he could get the swatches.

"Mother Fiddlestadt, we know you love your animals," Butch used a calm voice, "but really? I own a hardware store. No one lets their animals choose their house colors."

"Well, this is Fuchsia," Silas countered, "Nothing here makes sense as far as I can tell. That's what makes life here interesting."

George came back with the color swatches. Mavis took them out of his hands and spread them over the lawn.

Granny turned to the shysters and the cohorts. "Find your colors."

The animals didn't move; they just stared up at Granny.

"See," Penelope pointed out, "They don't know what you're talking about."

A grunt came from under the tree. Mr. Porkster got up and waddled over to a pink swatch and sat down on top of it.

The shysters and the cohorts, seeing what Mr. Porkster had done, spread out over the colors. Little White Poodle sat by Mr. Porkster as did Fish. Baskerville picked a bright blue swatch. Tank sniffed around and finally sat down on red. Furball examined the blue and then settled on a neon green swatch.

"Now what?" Penelope shook her head in disbelief that they were actually trying to let animals select their color scheme.

Silas spoke up, "Narrow it down to the ones they're sitting on and have them choose again from among those."

Butch laughed. "Silas, you can't believe in this hoo-ha."

Silas picked up the other swatches.

Granny laughed and said to the animals, "Choose."

"Can we choose too?" Mavis asked. "This is fun. It's like a cakewalk at a carnival."

Baskerville looked at all the colors as did the rest of the animals. They all ended up sitting on neon green.

"Neon green in Fuchsia?" Mavis wondered.

"Why not?" George asked. "We don't have a neon green house in this neighborhood. The rest of your house is a little boring too, Granny. It's still the gray it was when you bought it. Never understood someone painting a house gray; it's the only gray house in town."

"Thanks, folks, for your help!" Woodly Spackle hollered down from his ladder.

"Forgot you were up there, Woodly!" Granny yelled back. "I guess you need to change the color of the addition to neon green. While you're at it, when you're done, I need you to paint the rest of the house too. We'll decide the color later."

"You got it, Granny!" Woodly began to tear off the siding he'd already put on the house.

The shysters and the cohorts happily took off down the street. Mr. Pigster went back under the tree for a snooze.

Penelope shook her head. "Maybe you should wait with the color since you and Franklin are getting married in August and you and Franklin are moving into his Victorian house. Let the next owner paint this house."

Granny ignored the advice. "Thanks, everyone! Got things to do now. See you later!" Granny thought for a moment. "Mavis, can I have a word with you in the house?"

"Sure. George, I'll be right home so we can start our new script."

Safe in the house so no one would overhear their conversation, Granny said to Mavis, "They arrested

Jack Puffleman for Justine's murder. He didn't do it. We have to go to the chocolate factory and see if we can find something that they missed. Amelia will let us in. You call the rest of the gals. Midnight in the underground street! Tell Lulu to bring her van and have it parked at the Pink Percolator. We'll pick up Amelia and then head to the chocolate factory. Tell no one else."

"George is going home to his family in Iowa tonight for a few days," said Mavis, "so I won't have to figure a way to buffalo him. I'll call the girls. Where were you today, Granny? I saw your car leave around 11:30."

"You saw my car leave and you didn't stop it?" Granny admonished Mavis.

"You wanted me to stop you from leaving?" Mavis shook her head, confused.

"It wasn't me! It was Gram Gramstead!"

"I heard Gram was dead. Maybe you've been under too much stress planning this wedding with Franklin."

"I'm not under any stress." Granny's voice got louder, "Mavis, you know me! The only stress I have is how to dress. Now, go call everyone. I have a couple of phone calls to make."

"I'm off, I'm off!" Mavis danced out the door.

"You're off, alright," Granny muttered to the wall.

Picking up her phone, she called Ditty Belle, "Ditty, do you have a history book of the families of Brilliant?"

Granny could hear Ditty thinking out loud on the other end, "Do I? Do I? Do I?"

"That's three 'Do I's.' How about an 'I do'?" Granny barked through the phone.

"You have 'I do's on the mind," Ditty Belle teased, "Anxious to marry Franklin? Did you really call it off, like Amelia said in church?"

"No, I did not. That's Amelia, always deciphering what I say wrong. Back to the subject, do you have that book?"

"I'll find it. What are you looking for?"

"A family by the name of Carissa and Doug Melborne. We think they adopted Amelia's son."

"I'll get right on it." The line went dead.

Granny decided to make some coffee and have a donut. Looking at the counter, she frowned when she saw that her donuts were gone. All that was left were crumbs. Those darn shysters and cohorts! Baskerville must have gotten them down for the rest of the crew. She'd have to find a hiding place that they couldn't get to.

Granny lifted up the pet dishes to grab a piece of candy from her hiding place under the dishes only to find empty candy wrappers. Had they found those too? She traveled the hallway to her bedroom to get a piece of candy out of her hidden closet when she noticed her umbrella and her knitting needle cane were missing. Had she left them somewhere? She remembered that she must not have brought them up from the room by the underground street when she'd left with the girls the other night.

Walking down the basement steps, she picked up more candy wrappers. Examining the wrapper as she walked, she noticed the name on the wrapper—Gritty Gumdrops. She never had Gritty Gumdrops; she only ate chocolate. Maybe the shysters had gotten them from Angel. She'd have to talk to Thor. Gritty Gumdrops were no candy for children.

Flicking the switch for the fireplace door, she entered the room that led to the underground street. Her umbrella and knitting needle cane were nowhere to be found.

Granny checked the door. It was unlocked. Had she left it unlocked? Granny looked around; nothing else seemed out of place. She locked the door and went back through the fireplace door and locked it. Carefully, she looked around her downstairs. It appeared to be as she'd left it when she'd last cleaned.

Going back upstairs, she looked around her living room. The drawer in her old hutch was slightly ajar. She went to close it when she noticed a piece of paper stuck in the drawer. It had writing on it. "By hook or by crook, by skew or brew, by snow or woe, I'm your foe! I know where you go, your days are few because I'm going to get you!"

"Someone has been here," Granny said to the air as she turned the note over in her hand. She didn't recognize the writing. She stuffed the note in her pocket. She'd show it to the girls later. Picking up her phone, she texted the women that forks were needed. "Go see Hotdish," she added. "She'll know what you need. Bring them with you tonight."

CHAPTER THIRTY-SEVEN

The underground streets were deserted when Ditty Belle, Mavis and Granny met at midnight to make their way to the Pink Percolator. Delight was waiting to let them in. A soft light from the kitchen glowed in the background, lighting their way into the coffee house.

"I didn't want to turn on the lights because I didn't want to alert anyone that we were here," Delight explained the dimly lit restaurant.

"I have some news for Amelia," Ditty Belle told Granny.

"Humboldt said he had news for Amelia too when I saw him earlier this evening," Delight chimed in, "but he wanted to check with Silas first."

Delight peeked out the back door. "Lulu's here! Come on."

"Did you all purchase your forks from Hotdish?" asked Granny. "Maybe I should have had you stop by the hardware store and purchase pitchforks too." Granny held up her pink pitchfork. "But I thought Butch and Penelope might get suspicious."

"Where's Pastor Henrietta?" Mavis asked. "Isn't she coming with us?"

"She called," Delight whispered as they made their way to the van. She'll meet us at Amelia's. She had to stop at the jail. There was an emergency with Jack Puffleman and they needed a pastor."

"He didn't do it!" Granny proclaimed.

"Get in!" Lulu motioned for the women to hop in the van.

"Thanks for bringing your van, Lulu; they might have recognized mine. Watch out! I see one of Fuchsia's finest down the block. See, you can see the light's flashing," Ditty Belle pointed out.

"Looks like they have a car pulled over," Lulu concluded. As she pulled the van slowly out of the alley, she killed the lights.

"Lulu, you can drive with no headlights?" Delight's concerned voice echoed Mavis thoughts.

"Ooh, we're going to shine the deer, hit the wall, die in the dark!" Mavis's scared voice pierced through the darkness.

"We're going one block and she's going to turn the corner. I'm going to fire all of you from helping me sleuth out crime if you don't all keep it together," Granny threatened her friends.

Lulu turned at the corner and flicked on the lights and then proceeded to Amelia's house. Amelia and Pastor Henrietta came out of the shadows at the corner of the house and quickly got in the van. A siren could be heard in the background.

Granny turned as she saw the shadow of a flashing light through an alley they passed by. "Something's going on. Quick! Pull over behind that tree and cut the lights."

"How did you get away from the Pink Percolator since it's down the street from the police and fire station?" Amelia asked.

"We used the alley and went the opposite direction. The back of the police and fire station open into a different alley," Delight explained.

"Maybe we should see what's going on," Ditty Belle nervously suggested.

"Maybe there's another murder," Mavis's voice shook.

"The sirens are heading the other way. We need to go on. I need answers to where my son is and why Robert died," Amelia stubbornly reminded them.

"They're gone now," Granny deduced.

Lulu started the van again and pulled out, checking to make sure the coast was clear. They made it to the parking lot of the factory without anyone seeing them.

"Park the van around the corner from the office. It'll be hidden there," said Amelia. "I had a little nook and patio built outside of my office where I could relax, but where I also could park my car so I could sneak in and get some work done and they wouldn't know I was there." Amelia pointed in the direction Lulu should drive.

Lulu parked the van and the women piled out, waiting silently as Amelia unlocked the door to her office.

Once inside, Amelia turned the lights on in her office. "No one can see us back here."

The women looked around. "Amelia, this is so you," Granny remarked.

"Wowser, this is a perfect reality TV show setting." Mavis said, as she wandered around touching the plush furniture.

"This is spa-like," Ditty Belle added and touched the water flowing from a fountain.

"It's an oasis of calm," Pastor Henrietta reflected as she whirled around, taking in the entire large space.

Amelia nodded her head. "Running a company is stressful at times so in every factory or office space, I always have my own oasis where I can relieve my stress and still work. The only person allowed in here is Lars. Make yourself comfortable, ladies, while we decide what we're looking for."

"Got any wine, Amelia?" Granny asked, "Might make us think better."

"Or see things that aren't there," Mavis piped in, thinking of a scene for a reality show.

Amelia got out the wine that was in her wine cabinet and poured a glass for each of them.

Granny addressed Ditty Belle, "Tell us what you found out, Ditty Belle," and turning to Amelia, she explained, "I had Ditty Belle see if she had a book that listed the former families of Brilliant."

Amelia turned to Ditty Belle with a look of hope in her eyes. "Did you find anything?"

"I did. I found a woman by the name of Carissa Shultz Melborne. She lived in Brilliant about the same time that you were married to Robert." Ditty Belle showed the piece of paper to Amelia.

"Did they mention a child?" Amelia asked.

"No, at the time this book was published there was no child. This company quit putting together books like this not too long after this date though. I'm sorry."

Amelia hung her head.

"But, Ditty Belle continued, "I can tell you that Carissa Shultz Melborne was born Carissa Blackford, married Melvin Shultz and when he died she married Douglas Melborne."

"She must have been Robert's sister." Granny shook her head. "The love of my life never told me he had a sister."

"So where are Carissa and Douglas Melborne now?" Amelia wondered.

"Douglas Melborne is dead. Died a few years after they were married. I was able to find that out," Ditty Belle told the women.

"Humboldt said he had news but had to tell Silas first. Wasn't he going to go to Brilliant to see if he could find them," Delight reminded the group.

"We're getting away from why we're here. We have to clear Jack Puffleman." Granny brought the subject back to the matter at hand.

"It's nice and quiet here," Pastor Henrietta noted. "Not like at the hospital."

"Jack Puffleman. Emergency," Granny stated. "What was the emergency, Henrietta? Is Jack okay?"

Pastor Henrietta shook her head. "It's wait and see. He had a heart attack at the jail. He's at the Fuchsia hospital now. It's strange because he had no history of heart problems. They found him in his cell. Maybe the stress of his daughter's death and being arrested for it was just too much for him. I said a few prayers by his bedside with his wife."

"Amelia, how can we get out into the factory where Justine was found without being seen from the outside?"

"Not a problem. Didn't you notice when we were there? No windows, all skylights. And the skylights have shades. I want my workers to be comfortable so the shades can be adjusted if the sun gets too bright. Then we have a panel on the side of the factory workrooms that roll away and let in light. The panels can be shut and we can close the skylight shades and turn on the lights."

"Well, let's go!" Granny popped up from her seat and headed for the door.

Amelia caught up to Granny and led the way, adjusting the shades and the lights. They reached the room where the large chocolate vat was.

Granny gazed at the large stirring vat. "That's lot of chocolate to taste."

Amelia laughed. "It's going to be a big operation."

The other women were suspiciously silent.

Ditty Belle tried to speak but nothing came out of her mouth. She moved and took Mavis's hand.

Lulu moved over to join the two women. Pastor Henrietta, seeing that the women seemed to be experiencing some kind of quiet emotion spoke, "It's hard to believe we lost Justine right here. I didn't know her, but I'm sure she's here with us in spirit. Maybe we can feel her spirit and she'll tell us something."

They heard a noise. The women jumped closer together. Granny and Amelia both moved their gaze to the office door. Granny held up her pitchfork."

Pastor Henrietta coughed nervously. "Well, I didn't actually mean that Justine's ghost was here."

Amelia mouthed to Granny, "I have the key."

Amelia moved closer to the door. Granny stood in position to go in with her pitchfork when the door was unlocked and opened. The other women nervously held up their large barbeque forks.

Amelia counted quietly, "1..2..3" and turned the key in the lock. Granny pushed open the door and hit a tae-kwon-do pose with her fork in front of her, hollering "Hi Yah!"

A scream rent the air.

"What? Aaah, Granny! You scared us half to death! What are you doing here?"

Granny, seeing Lars and Ella, put the fork down. "I think the question is what you're doing here and what *are* you doing?" noting their disheveled clothing.

"Is that Ella I hear?" Delight pushed her way past Granny. "Ella, I want an explanation right now!"

"So do I!" Amelia's no-nonsense tone wasn't lost on Lars.

Lars stammered, "I can explain."

Granny held up her pitchfork. "I think you'd better explain to my daughter Starshine, Lars. You remember her—the one who's wearing your engagement ring!"

Pastor Henrietta squeezed past Granny, Amelia and Delight. "Okay, let's all calm down! We need peace in the world; we need to learn to forgive and love one another. Let's all go back to Amelia's spa-like office and breath in calmness and sort this out."

Ditty Belle could be heard from the back of the pack, "I'll get the wine!"

CHAPTER THIRTY-EIGHT

"This better be good," Granny informed Lars.

Amelia looked at her sister. "Hermiony, I'm sure there's a good explanation for this."

"Or he's got you hoodwinked, Amelia. Maybe he's Justine's killer—after all, he found her!"

Ditty Belle and Lulu nodded their heads in agreement. Mavis tipped up her wine glass and waited to see what would happen next.

"Ella, tell your mother what you're doing here. Now!" Delight's tone held none of her giggly personality.

"Lars's sheepish look stayed on his face as he spoke, "I'm not really engaged to Starshine. She's engaged to someone else, but isn't quite ready to have you meet him, so since we're friends, she talked me into pretending to be her fiancé." He paused, waiting for a reaction from Granny and when there was none, he continued, "I was seeing Justine. That's why she had a key to the factory. We would meet here at night. I couldn't let anyone know I was seeing her because I was pretending to be engaged to Starshine. Justine knew this. Then I fell in love with Ella." He smiled at Ella, but noticing Delight's glare, continued his story. "I was going to tell Justine that night. She texted me and told me she'd gotten my text about meeting her here at the factory. I hadn't texted her yet so I was mystified. I came to find her and gently break the truth to her, but when I got here she was dead. That's all I know. I told the police the truth except for the fact that I was seeing both Justine and Ella. I didn't want to drag Ella into this."

"Do you think it was it Jack Puffleman who texted Justine?" Granny suggested.

Lars shook his head. "No, she'd just seen him and he'd just found out that he was Justine's father. He didn't take it well, but she was killed in the factory shortly after she saw him. I know because I saw him through the show window of AbStract after Justine left. I knew she went there to tell him that he was her father and I wanted to catch her afterwards so we could talk. But then she got that text she thought was from me and went straight o the factory. She must have left by another door."

"Did you send me this note?" Granny handed him the note she'd found at her house.

Lars shook his head after reading the note. "No, why would I send you a note like this? I don't want you dead. You're my new aunt."

"Dead?" Mavis chirped, grabbing the note from Granny.

"Note?" Lulu grabbed the note out of Granny's hand. She read it and passed the note to Henrietta.

"Oh my, oh my!" Pastor Henrietta raised her eyes to the ceiling and said a silent prayer.

"What are you all talking about?" Amelia took the note from Henrietta while Delight looked over her shoulder and read the note too. "We should call your husband."

"Husband? You and Franklin got married and you didn't invite me?" Mavis scolded.

"You married Franklin and Granny and didn't tell us?" Ditty Belle accused Pastor Henrietta.

Pastor Henrietta shook her head. "I didn't marry Franklin and Granny."

Granny held up her hands to silence everyone and used her loud voice, "Enough! We're getting off the subject."

"Call your husband, Silas; he needs to know about this," Amelia spoke up again.

Granny turned to Amelia. "He's not my husband. Remember, or did you forget that it was a fake ceremony so we could find out information about your son?" Granny stomped her pitchfork on the ground to make a point.

The sound of the pitchfork and Granny's words silenced the room. Lars grabbed Ella during the commotion and slipped out unnoticed through the door to Amelia's private patio.

Amelia stepped up to Granny and stood face-to-face with her, "Well, actually my plan worked and you are married to Silas! And I'm going to marry Franklin—he just doesn't know it yet!"

The onlookers gasped at Amelia's words.

Granny's body pulled itself up straight and stiffened; she held her pitchfork tighter, "You did it again, Amelia! You stole my fiancé and hooked me up to a conniving, cantankerous old coot! How did you do it? Here I was, willing to help you find your son and you double-crossed me! Did you have the information about the adoption all along?" Granny's voice got louder with each sentence.

Amelia, too, pulled herself up to her full height. "No! Hermiony, I did you a favor when I ran away with Robert. Look at the life you would have had. He was a conniving crook! He stole my son. You had a husband and family that took care of you. I lost my parents, my family and my son. Anyone with two eyes can see that you belong with Silas. Franklin's too controlling for you, but he's perfect for me. You're too ornery to see it for yourself, so I had to trick you into this. The judge gave me the adoption information when I came in and arranged the ruse. I do need your help, but I'm saving you from your stubborn self. If there's anything I learned in the corporate world it's that you get what you want with a little sugar and a little vinegar—and this is the vinegar!" Amelia took a breath and sat down on the sofa.

Everyone in the room held their breath waiting for the outburst they knew would come.

Granny stood still for a moment, her expressions changing and then becoming unreadable. She looked at the others in the room. They began to clap. Wide smiles lit up their faces.

Granny sat down next to her sister. Shaking her head, she acknowledged, "It's possible that I could like Silas a little bit. Maybe you're right about Franklin and me, Amelia. I have been blessed." Granny sat for a moment longer before leaning over and giving Amelia a hug. "But I have missed one thing—my sister."

Amelia looked up, and with tears running down her cheeks, she hugged her sister.

The others in the room clapped louder.

"More wine for everyone! "Mavis announced.

"Does Silas know?" Granny asked Amelia.

Amelia shook her head. "No, I was waiting for the right time to break it to both of you—and then Franklin."

A sound at the door to the factory caught their attention. The door burst open and Granny saw a flash of red before she saw the gun being pointed at all of them.

Granny stood up, holding her pitchfork in front of her. "Sonny Boy!"

The man with the gun leered at Granny. "Thought you'd never see me again, didn't you? My mother's dead! She died of a broken heart in prison—all because of you!"

"Sonny Boy, it was you who stole my car and tried to run me down, not your mother," Granny said as she moved over in front of Amelia.

Sonny Boy waved the gun around the room, targeting all of them. "You're right! It *was* me! Loved your house! Great donuts, by the way. Are you missing any weapons? Put the pitchfork down, Granny, I'm on to you. Gently! So I don't have to shoot you too soon. I don't want to harm the rest of them. I figure I'm going back to prison anyway. My mother's funeral provided me the perfect escape. The rest of you can go—out that door. Go on!" he waved the gun at them."

"Go," Granny said. "I can handle myself."

Pastor Henrietta stepped forward. "I'm not leaving. I will be protected."

Mavis, Ditty Belle and Delight murmured to each other. They linked arms and refused to leave. "All for one and one for all!"

"Fine! Suit yourselves and sit down and be quiet." Sonny Boy turned his attention back to Granny. "Hard to believe there are two of you. Although from what I've observed, she's a little bit wimpy." He gestured toward Amelia.

Sonny Boy laughed at Amelia's expression. "Yah, I know all about you. I met Dickey Lee Hatchet in prison and he told me about this woman who pretended to be her sister and pulled the wool over his brother's eyes. I didn't put two and two together until he broke out of prison and contacted me. Then my mother died. I wanted revenge. It's your entire fault. You ruined everything for us, Granny. When he told me where he was, I knew I had to be here. Told me he and his brother were holed up in an old basement that everyone had forgotten about. So after I knocked off my guard at my mother's funeral—they wouldn't even let her be buried back here in Fuchsia in some forgotten cemetery in New York—I knew where I was headed."

Mavis's voice interrupted his story, "Did you kill that Dickey Lee too?"

"Did I hear a voice from the quiet corner?" he snarled, waving his gun. "Maybe I'll change my mind about letting you all live!"

Delight's soft voice answered him, "Well, if we're going to die, please, we want to know."

Sonny Boy laughed at Delight's soft voice, "Well, since it was your forest I stole a few years ago, I guess I can give you an answer. Yes, I killed him and that brother of his too."

Amelia gasped. "You killed Robert? He didn't die of a heart attack?"

"Nope, an injection, but the police know that," said Sonny boy as he looked at Granny. "But that detective son of yours didn't tell you that, did he?"

Pastor Henrietta stood up. "What did you do to Jack Puffleman?"

"Sit back down, sister." A laugh erupted from Sonny Boy "Sorry, wrong religion!"

"He saw me that night but didn't realize it right away. He recognized me from when I was dating Estelle. Justine did though and that's why I had to lure her here. I've been watching all of Fuchsia right under their eyes. Those small town cops were looking all over for me but they had no idea I was hiding right under their noses here in the chocolate factory."

"You were hiding in my factory!" Amelia exclaimed.

"It's a big place. I stole the key from Justine. She thought she lost it. I let myself in and out at night as I pleased. Stole the key on the wall too and planted it on Justine's body. I made sure it had Jack Puffleman's fingerprints all over it. You did see a woman with a red wig driving your car, Granny. I dressed in disguise like a woman, but I changed my wig when I was out in public." He plucked a blonde wig out of his pocket and plunked it on his head.

Delight gasped, as did Ditty Belle and Lulu. "I know you! You have the triple chocolate latté with a dollop of whipped crème on top."

An evil grin lit up Sonny Boy's face. "You got it. You were my test. I passed when you didn't recognize me. But the night Justine and Jack Puffleman saw me I didn't have my disguise on."

"Granny frowned. "But why kill Dickey Lee and Robert and switch their identities?"

"You ask too many questions, Granny. I think it's time for your questioning to end." He pointed the gun straight at Granny. A gasp came up from the back of the room. Amelia stood up and moved toward Sonny Boy. "No, don't kill her yet. Let her know why first, then kill her."

Another gasp came from the corner of the room.

"Thanks, Amelia, how touching. Apparently, you still hold a grudge because Robert preferred me over you." Granny winked at her sister.

"That's right. I'm glad Robert's dead. You did me a favor when you killed him, but tell me why you wanted him dead, Sonny Boy—if that's your name." Amelia nodded that he should continue.

Keeping his gun pointed at Granny, Sonny boy thought for a minute before continuing, "It's kind of a fun story. Ol' Dickey Lee and Robert didn't like my plan to off Granny here; it seems Robert still had a little yen for the old woman."

At the words *old woman*, Granny moved over a bit and gently stepped on the pitchfork handle while holding his attention with her eyes so he wouldn't notice.

"They were going to give themselves up and tell the police," he said. "Seems the only thing they were interested in was finding Robert's son and they weren't having any luck anyway. Ol' Robert was in the silo. I injected a little hard to detect substance and he had a heart attack—worked great on Jack Puffleman too. I killed his brother after Robert died, because he was still going to go to the police and turn himself in. I couldn't let him do that. Did I tell you I'm good with a knife?" Sonny Boy's cackle filled the room.

"Tell me where my son is and then you can kill her," Amelia ordered.

Granny turned her head and nodded to the women in the corner. They looked confused at her nod but nodded back.

"Sorry," Sonny Boy said to Amelia, "but don't know; don't care. It's time to put your sister out of her misery. The rest of you back there might want to shut your eyes because I know I'm not getting out of here. I want to be with my mother. Granny goes first," he said, prodding the gun at Granny, "and I go next!"

At the word *next*, Granny and Amelia let loose with a fake faint. The faint was enough to detract Sonny Boy. The women in the corner jumped up with their BBQ forks ready to attack, but Granny had quickly grabbed her pitchfork and knocked the gun out of Sonny Boy's hands. Both the door to the factory and the patio burst open. The room filled with policemen with the Tall Guy and Thor leading the charge.

Granny looked up from the floor "'Bout time you guys got here! What! No shysters or cohorts to help you?"

Thor helped his mother off the floor and the Tall Guy did the same for Amelia. The police hustled the other women out the back door while Franklin and Silas came in the front door.

"Woman, you are going to be the death of us yet—or worse yet, the death of you!" Silas scolded.

Franklin hugged Granny and Amelia at the same time in one giant bear hug. "Amelia, what did your sister talk you into this time? Hermiony, I can't take much more of this; trouble seems to find you or you find trouble. We can't be married soon enough."

Granny eyed Amelia to see if she was going to spill the secret.

Amelia extracted herself from the bear hug and saw her stepson coming through the back door. He moved towards her and scooped her up in his arms "I should have told you I'm sorry."

Amelia patted him on the chest. "We'll talk about this later."

"Aren't you supposed to be home with my new grandson?" Granny said to Thor.

"Well, I could be but someone called me and told me my mother was in trouble again. I have to call home; your daughters are both at my house waiting for news." Reaching for his cell phone, he moved outside to make the call.

"I suppose you want our statement," Granny said, approaching the Tall Guy.

"No, we heard it all. Lars and Ella were on the patio when Ella recognized Sonny Boy through the blinds and saw what was happening; they called us. We were already out looking for Sonny Boy. We've known for weeks that he'd escaped and was looking for you, Granny, but we decided to not tell you so you wouldn't get in trouble trying to find him. We were out looking for him tonight. He was spotted earlier."

Granny commented, "I guess that plan worked well; you should have Amelia plot out your plans."

"What?"

"Finish your story."

"There's an intercom system here. We were right outside waiting for the right moment to come in. Lars activated the system so we could hear what was happening. We heard Sonny Boy's entire confession. He's going away for a long time."

The Tall Guy nodded to Franklin and Silas. "Take these women home. It's 3:00 a.m. and past their bedtime. The other women have already left."

"I'm kind of getting used to these late night meetings," Granny stated as they left Amelia's office.

"Not me," Amelia said, "I like my beauty sleep."

"You always did sleep through life." Granny gave Amelia a playful jab on the arm.

Amelia laughed, "Until I left home."

"Glad something I taught ya when you were home carried you through."

Franklin shook his head. "Well, Crickett, I guess we didn't do such a bad job working together keeping these two safe. Maybe we don't make a bad team." He turned to Silas to shake his hand. "Thank you for helping me keep my fiancé safe."

"Till the next time, Gatsby, with that one," he said, nodding at Granny. "Believe me, there'll always be a next time."

Franklin shook his head. "Nope, our wedding's coming up and nothing will stop us this time. I have plans for the future."

Granny paused and looked at her sister before commenting on Franklin's words, "Well, Franklin, you know what they say about the best laid plans."

CHAPTER THIRTY-NINE

Granny paced the floor waiting for Amelia to arrive. She took a sip of wine, followed by a sip of coffee, followed by a bite of a donut, followed by a piece of chocolate. Little White Poodle, Fish, Furball, Tank, Baskerville, Mrs. Bleaty and Mr. Pigster watched the back and forth movement that was uncharacteristic of their owner.

Amelia rang the doorbell and walked in, not waiting for Granny to answer. "What are you wearing?" she asked her sister.

Flip flops flipped and flopped as Granny paced. A purple hat adorned her head, a red chiffon blouse covered a pink t-shirt and they all topped her polyester granny skirt.

Granny looked down to see what she'd thrown on when she woke up after sleeping all day, catching up on her rest from being up the night before.

"Tell me I'm not married to Silas Crickett."

Amelia sat down on the couch. "I can't tell you that because you are."

"I want a divorce. I have to have a divorce; my marriage to Franklin is coming up soon. How could you do this?"

"Hermiony, I told you why I did it. I am the voice of reason here."

"You want to steal Franklin from me so you arranged this scam."

"Yes, yes, I do want to marry Franklin."

"What happened while he was keeping his eye on you?" Granny stopped pacing long enough to look Amelia straight in the eyes.

"Nothing, nothing; that's the problem. He thinks he wants to marry you. But, Hermiony, you won't be happy. He has a lot of Ferdinand in him. He likes his way and I like that. I had to do it."

"What's Silas going to say? He doesn't want to be married to me anymore than I want to be married to him."

"We have to tell them. I've asked Pastor Henrietta to come over while we do it."

"What? Why?"

"Trust me," Amelia said with a sly grin.

Granny was about to respond when the doorbell rang.

Amelia instructed, "Now, go back there and get dressed in something different. Something like I'm wearing."

The doorbell rang again. Amelia called out, "Just a minute! Coming!"

Granny looked at Amelia. "You're dressed like I usually dress."

Amelia smiled, "Exactly. No more questions, get dressed."

Granny was going to argue, but was curious about this new side of Amelia. As Amelia answered the door, Granny heard the shysters and the cohorts' door swishing. They too were home.

Mr. Pigster, sleeping under Granny's bed, gave a snort and went back to sleep, not caring that there was a live person in the room or that barks, bleats and meows were coming from the living room.

When Granny joined Amelia back in the living room, Franklin was there along with Pastor Henrietta and Silas.

Amelia came over to greet Granny, winking at her so that the others couldn't see and said, "Amelia, about time you showed up! Sure takes you a long time to get gussied up."

Granny looked at Amelia, moving her eyes around the room, skeptically wondering what Amelia had up her sleeve. This wasn't the Amelia she remembered. "Ah, yes, took a little longer than I expected. Silas, Franklin, Pastor Henrietta. So, uh Granny," Hermiony put a heavy accent on the word *Granny* when addressing Amelia, "what are we all doing here?"

"I have an announcement to make. Franklin, don't say anything until I'm done. Understand!"

"You're in trouble, Franklin," Silas spouted, followed by a scowl from Amelia. "What? You didn't say I couldn't say anything!"

Amelia, still pretending to be Granny continued, "I can't wait to marry you, Franklin; we've waited too long. What if another murder or kidnapping creeps up or they decide to close down the Fuchsia underground streets. It would delay our marriage, so I've asked Pastor Henrietta here to perform the ceremony. Silas and Amelia can be our witnesses."

"Well, ah, ah, what about the marriage license?" Franklin sputtered.

"All taken care of," Pastor Henrietta said, stepping forward. "Sign here." She left the top part of the paper covered.

"Well, maybe we should wait for our families. They might feel bad," said Franklin.

"Franklin, do you want to marry me or not? We're getting married today. Sign that paper!"

Franklin swallowed and could barely be heard saying, "Fine." He took the pen and signed the paper.

"Shall we begin?" Pastor Henrietta asked.

"Yes, but cut out all the stuff except for the 'I do's. We were almost there the last time before I got kidnapped," Amelia sounded exactly like her sister.

"Do you, Franklin, take this woman to be your wife, to have and to hold from this day forward, for better, for worse, in sickness and in health? Please say *I do*."

Franklin looked deep into Granny/Amelia's eyes and said, "I do."

"Do you," Pastor Henrietta nodded at Amelia, "take Franklin to be your wedded husband, to have and to hold from this day forward, for better, for worse, in sickness and in health?"

Amelia looked deep into Franklin's eyes and said, "I do."

Pastor Henrietta continued, "I now pronounce you man and wife. You may kiss the bride."

Franklin gathered Amelia in his arms. He set her back apart from him and said, "Amelia, no more pretending to be Hermiony as long as we're married."

Amelia jumped back out of his arms, "You knew?"

"You married her anyway and you knew?" Granny jumped forward. "You were supposed to be marrying me!" Granny ranted.

Silas and Franklin exchanged a look and laughed.

"It would be awfully hard to marry you when you're married to Silas," said Franklin.

Granny turned to Silas. "You knew?" She then turned to Amelia. "You told me he didn't know."

Amelia shrugged. "I didn't tell him."

The animals quietly took in the scene. Baskerville put his paws over his eyes. Mrs. Bleaty nibbled on the flowers that were still there from Granny's wedding to Silas. The rest of the animals left the living room to retreat under the bed in Granny's room, waiting for the eruption of the Granny volcano.

"I told him," Silas announced. "I noticed the wedding license that I signed with Granny was the real deal. I also know the judge so after the ceremony I had old Snowshoe go back over and check it out. I was wondering when you were going to reveal the entire plan, Amelia."

"And this is okay with you?" Granny questioned.

"Mrs. Persnickulous, my ornery, crabby lady. I've been trying to tell you for the past year that you belong with me, not Franklin. I knew you'd wake up to it sooner or later, but hay! When Amelia has a plan, she has a plan!"

Amelia looked Franklin in the eyes and asked, "And you, Franklin?"

"Well, I didn't see your plan, but when Silas told me what had happened and I thought about how much I enjoyed the time I'd spent with you, I realized this was maybe meant to be, and then in a light bulb moment today, when you arranged this ceremony, I knew that I did want to marry you."

Franklin turned to Granny. "I love you, Hermiony; I always will, but as a sister-in-law. This woman, your sister, saw what none of us could see. I hope you'll forgive me."

Granny looked at Silas. "No rats, you understand. Squeaky has to go elsewhere. Got that?"

Before Silas could answer, the doorbell rang and Ditty Belle, Mavis, Delight and Lulu let themselves in.

"Did we interrupt something?" Delight asked, not waiting for an answer. "Ditty Belle has exciting news!"

"You found out something about my son?" asked Amelia.

"Better than that!" Lulu answered for Ditty Belle.

"She teamed up with Humboldt Snowshoe Notorious and they found your son!" Delight announced excitedly.

"Yes, well, it seems that Carissa Blackford Shultz Melborne remarried and relocated to Fuchsia. Carissa Blackford Shultz Melborne ultimately married Terrence Trawler."

The door opened and Humboldt Notorious ushered a man into the room. "Let me introduce you to your son, Amelia—Tricky Travis Blackford Trawler!"

The End.

Other Books by Julie Seedorf

Fuchsia, Minnesota, series

Granny Hooks A Crook
Granny Skewers A Scoundrel
Granny Snows A Sneak

Granny's in Trouble series

Whatchamacallit? Thingamajig?
Snicklefritz

Collection of Julie Seedorf's *Something About Nothing* Columns

Something About Nothing published by Hermiony Vidalia Books

Stories in anthologies

We Go on: Charity Anthology For Veterans published by Kiki Howel

ABOUT THE AUTHOR

Author Julie Seedorf is a columnist, author and dreamer. She lived her live as a wife and mom, experiencing various careers including that of computer technician, retiring from her computer repair business in January of 2014, to follow her dream and transition to that of full-time writer.

Beside her Fuchsia, Minnesota series, she is the author of the Granny's In Trouble Series bringing mystery to the life of young readers along with sharing who Granny is under the wrinkles, so her grandchildren will always know that Granny can be forever young. Her column *Something About Nothing*, is written with the idea that under the nothings we all talk about there is a hidden something waiting to get out. Julie is a longtime Minnesota resident who shares the tough Minnesota winters with her Granny character. Outside of writing she likes to read, try new hobbies and scurries to keep up with her social media. She lives with her husband and has two shysters of her own, Borris and Natasha. Her favorite moments are those she spends with her friends and family, especially her grandchildren.

Visit Julie at http://julieseedorf.com
Her blog: http://sprinklednotes.com
Facebook: http://www.facebook.com/julie.seedorf.author
Twitter: julieseedorf@julieseedorf
Pinterest: Julie Seedorf, Author
Instagram: Julie Seedorf
Amazon Author Page: amazon.com/author/julieseedorf

WITHDRAWN

$14.95

LONGWOOD PUBLIC LIBRARY
800 Middle Country Road
Middle Island, NY 11953
(631) 924-6400
longwoodlibrary.org

LIBRARY HOURS

Monday-Friday   9:30 a.m. - 9:00 p.m.
Saturday   9:30 a.m. - 5:00 p.m.
Sunday (Sept-June) 1:00 p.m. - 5:00 p.m.

53967403R00151

Made in the USA
Middletown, DE
30 November 2017